THE GUY
NEXT DOOR

BRENDA L. CARRUTH

authorHOUSE®

AuthorHouse™
1663 Liberty Drive
Bloomington, IN 47403
www.authorhouse.com
Phone: 1 (800) 839-8640

Published by AuthorHouse   02/08/2018

ISBN: 978-1-5246-7454-0 (sc)
ISBN: 978-1-5246-7453-3 (e)

Library of Congress Control Number: 2017903227

Print information available on the last page.

Any people depicted in stock imagery provided by Thinkstock are models,
and such images are being used for illustrative purposes only.
Certain stock imagery © Thinkstock.

This book is printed on acid-free paper.

Because of the dynamic nature of the Internet, any web addresses or links contained in
this book may have changed since publication and may no longer be valid. The views
expressed in this work are solely those of the author and do not necessarily reflect the
views of the publisher, and the publisher hereby disclaims any responsibility for them.

Shorty a hidden forbidden true love.

Chapter 1

Ladies let me have your attention for a minute. You know how we get sometimes, when a tall good looking guy move right next door to us. We do everything we can to get his attention. Play the little mind games smile speak to him all the time, and every time you go outside and see him you have on something skimpy and sexy. Because we already know he gone look. He is a man. Even though he is married with two kids I didn't let that stop me because I'm the type of woman if I see something I'm going to get it whether he has a girlfriend, wife, fiancée, or pimping. That's how we do we love a challenge. And sometimes we get caught up in it. It start off as a game to us. But then sometimes we let our guards down and let our feelings get involved. That's when the problem start.

Let me tell you a little bit about me. My name is Shekela Baker. I was born and raised in Atlanta, Georgia. I'm 25 years old. I have a twin sister our relationship is OK, but it could be a whole lot better if she wasn't so bossy. Both of our parents are deceased. I'm smart educated I'm a nurse, and my sister Tekela is also a nurse. We both work the morning shift. We don't have any kids. It's so funny people can't tell us apart we are identical twins. We both are freaks. Short, sexy as hell, long hair, light brown eyes, kissable lips every man fantasy.

It's Friday about three thirty I'm just leaving work heading to the grocery store getting my shopping on. When I finished I headed home. As I was puling in the driveway look toward my right I seen a U-haul truck back in to the house next door. I seen a couple of kids of kids running around. When I got out of my truck, getting the groceries one of the bags fell apart. My food was going everywhere I bend down picking some of the things up. I heard this voice "You look like you could use some help." I raised up this tall sexy ass man out of no where came and help me. Well thank you. "It's my pleasure. I'm your new neighbor Antonio." Well how you doing Antonio I'm Shekela. You must be new in town I never seen you before. "As a matter of fact I am. We just moved from Dallas." We? "Yes me my wife and our two kids. You must work at a hospital I see you got your nurse uniform on." I do. "If you don't mind me asking what hospital?" AMG medical center. "Tell me you're joking." No. "What kind of nurse are you?" I'm an RN. "Well guess what." What's that? "We're going to see a lot of each other." Why is that? "Because I'm a doctor." A doctor. What kind of doctor? "I'm a heart surgeon, I start Monday morning." Wait a minute. Are you the same doctor I been hearing the women talk about. "They been talking about me?" Yes but trust me it's all good. "So tell me Shekela what have they been saying about me." It's just a couple of ladies saying we have a new doctor coming on board and how sexy he was, but I had no idea I was going to be living next door to the doctor. "Well is that a good thing or a bad thing?" Trust me it's all good. So where is the wife? "She won't be here for another two weeks." You mean to tell me she let you come to Atlanta by yourself for two weeks? "I'm a good boy." That's what they all say. We started laughing. "Well it's been a pleasure but I gotta go back to the house I got a lot of unpacking to do." So Doc if I had a heart attack, all I got to do is come next door and tell you. "I tell you one thing Shekela try not to have one, I'm just getting to know my new neighbor." Well I will try not to have one. "You do that." He walked away. Damn he got a nice ass on him. I grabbed my groceries and went into the house and started putting everything up. Went to the phone to check my messages. Called my sister and tell her everything that just happened. "You mean to tell me your lucky ass got a doctor living next door to you." Not just a doctor he is a heart surgeon. "Is he married?" Yes a couple of kids. "Shekela be careful." What are you talking about? "I know you. When you want something you go for it." Well you right about that because I love a challenge and he is sexy. Well I'm gone let you go so I can take a bath and go next door. "For what?" He just moving in I know he can use some help bye. When I finished talking to my sister I went upstairs and took a hot bubble bath. When I finished I put on a tight fitted t-shirt with no bra on so he could see my quarter nipple stick out, a pair of daisy duke short pants.

I went next door rung the door bell. When he opened the door he had a smile on his face. I came over to see did you need any help unpacking. "Well

I'm done for today. I'm gone take the kids out to get something to eat." Well that sound like a plan. I think I'm gone go do the same thing grab something to eat and come back and watch a movie. Well I hope you enjoy your first night in town. "Well thank you." As I was talking to him he couldn't take his eyes off my nipples. "Well you enjoy the rest of your day." You too. I slowly walked away, I knew he wasn't gone be able to take his eyes off my ass so I slowly turned around and smiled at him. I was right he had his eyes on my ass. I went into the house grabbed my keys got into my truck and went got some dinner.

When I made it back home I can see he was still out. His car wasn't in the driveway. I went inside climbed into bed started eating and watching TV. About twenty minutes later my phone rung. It was my two best friends Kiera and Alexandria. "We called to see what was you doing." Nothing just having dinner. Well let me tell you girls about my day. Would you believe me if I told you a doctor moved right next door. The first thing Kiera said "Is he sexy?" Girl yes he is. "And you ain't over there?" He is married with a couple of kids. Alexandria said "Have that ever stop you before?" No but trust and believe me I'm gone get that. So what are you ladies doing tonight. "Well we was calling you to see did you want to go to the club it's ladies night." What time are we going? "About Ten O'clock." Well who gone pick me up? "We gone all ride together." Well let me get up and start getting ready I'll see y'all when y'all get here. After I hung up with them I got up open up my closet looking for something sexy to put on. Since our houses was so close together I decided to open up the blinds so he could look right into bedroom. Since red is my favorite color I pulled out something erotic and sexy to put on. I went into my bathroom and did my makeup and pinned up my hair and got dressed. When I got finished I looked into the mirror. Damn I look so good right about now, it will make a blind man see and a cripple man walk. Only if he could see me right about now. He would definitely want to stick his dick in this, and believe me when I tell you this people I'm going to get that dick. It might take a lil time, but trust and believe me I'm gone fuck his head up. Only freaks can do that and everybody is not a freak.

It was about five minutes after ten I was downstairs waiting on my home girls to pick me up. A few minutes later I heard a horn outside, I looked out the window it was them. They got out and came in for minute. Kiera said "Damn Shekela what you trying to do make a man leave home tonight in that dress?" Not any man but the right man. As we walking out the door getting in the car Antonio came outside to take the trash out. He said "Well hey ladies." We spoke. He walked toward me "Where are you going dressed all up looking good?" We going to the club let me introduce you to my two best friends, this is Kiera and Alexandria. Ladies this is Antonio my new neighbor. Alexandria said "Damn maybe I should come get a house in the neighborhood. We began to laugh. "Well don't you ladies party to hard." We won't. We got in the car and drove off. Kiera said "Damn Shekela he couldn't take his eyes off of you." I know. "If you won't fuck him I will." Keep your coochie off my man. Alexandria said "Damn you ain't got the dick yet girl." Trust me in a matter of time I will be on that dick. "I know you ain't lying I feel sorry for him." Pussy, ass, and mouth is going to fuck his head totally up. Then the wife is going to have a problem. They said "Why you say that?" Because she won't be able to keep her man at home, and out of my pussy. "Damn Shekela you gone put the shit on a brother like that." You know how I get down, I don't have to ask or do nothing, because once I give it to him the first time best to believe he gone be back. Once he get a taste of this cream between my thighs he won't be able to stay away.

When we walk in Dream World all eyes was on us. We went to the bar and ordered some drinks. Sitting there laughing and talking. A couple of guys walked up and asked up did we want to dance. We did but the only thing was on my mind was fucking Antonio. We got our dance on, we got our drink, on we got our party on to bout three in the morning. As we were walking to the car a guy approach me and asked me could he have my phone number. Do you honestly except me to give you my phone number and I don't know you. "That's what women do when they come to the club give out their phone number to guys." Well let me explain something to you all women aren't hoes. "It doesn't make you a hoe if you give me your number." It will make me easy as hell. "Look liked all I want is the number so I can get to know you and take you out." Thank you but no thank you, I got my eye on something else. He walked away. We laughed about it. We got in the car and headed to my house. Kiera said "Damn Shekela he was fine." Girl I ain't even worried about that my mind is on something else right now and you already know what that is. "Yes we do we know you want to give the goodies to Antonio." You damn Skippy.

When we made it to my house I got out the car and said goodnight to the ladies. As I was walking up the steps looked toward the right I notice a couple of lights on in the house over there. So I'm assuming he still up so I hurried up got into the house ran upstairs, put on some soft music lit a couple of candles open the blinds wide open so he could look into my bedroom. I walked toward the window slowly starting undressing I slowly turned around and looked out the window. I was right he was up, looking dead at me all I had on was my stilettos and my red thong. I started rubbing my long nipples. He started sucking the bottom of his lip. I blew him a kiss he smiled at me. He moved away from the window a few minutes later he came back with a piece of paper in his hand and raised it up. I read it. The paper says "You are a bad girl I am scared of you." I grabbed a pen and paper and wrote "Don't be just come and play if you want to here's my number." When I finished I held it up. Moments later my phone rung. "Why are you doing this to me?" Because I like what I see, you mean to tell me you don't like all this. "I didn't say I didn't like what I see I'm a happily married man." Well I tell you what Antonio I won't tell if you won't. "A woman like you ain't nothing but temptation and a man like me can get in trouble for that. I'm trying to do the right thing." Sometimes the right thing ain't always the best thing to do." He started laughing. "Shekela please don't do this to me." I'm not gone do anything you don't want me to do. Why don't you just go back to the window and watch me play with my fat pussy lips. "Damn are they fat?" Come see for yourself. He went back to the window. I grabbed a chair and sat down spread my legs wide open took three of my fingers played with my pussy lips, pushed them in and out. The cum started dripping between my ass cheeks. His face lit up like Christmas. I slowly pulled my fingers out my pussy and put them into my mouth and started sucking on them. "Damn Shekela I can't take this shit no more open the door and let me in." I went downstairs and open the door he was standing right there. I grabbed him by his shirt and pulled him in closed the door behind him. I pushed him to the door. We started kissing. He started rubbing my ass cheeks telling me how good I smell. "Damn I can't believe I'm doing this." Do you want to stop? "Hell nawl, looking at them fat yellow pussy lips didn't do nothing but make my dick hard." What about your kids at home? "They sleep they will be OK, but I can't stay long." Well we got work to do. He pick me up carried me to the living room and laid me on the couch, spread my legs wide open started sucking on my nipples licking me on my stomach finger fucking me. I started moaning. He took his hand and put it in his mouth. "Damn you pussy taste so sweet." He put his head between my legs and begin to suck and pull on my fat pussy lips. He was eating the pussy so good I had cum all in his mouth. "I have never seen a woman cum the way you cum." You ain't seen nothing yet sweetie. He got undressed and laid back on the couch. I climbed on top of him started nibbling on his ear kissing on his neck. I placed my tongue in his mouth we started tongue kissing. I could feel his dick jumping up and down. I kissed him on his chest made my way down to the bottom of his dick. I took both of my hands and wrapped it around his dick. Damn he had a fat ass dick too. I place the head inside of my mouth started kissing and licking all on it. He began to moan calling my name. He took his hand and started pushing my head up and down on his dick. "Damn baby I ain't never had my dick sucked like this shit." I can feel his dick head hitting the back of my throat as I am swallowing his cum down like water. I can feel his legs shaking. After he pulled his dick out my mouth he couldn't wait to turn me over and get it from the back. "Wait a minute Shekela we gotta stop." Why? "Because I don't have a condom." Don't worry about it I'm a firm believer in safe sex. After he put the condom on he bend me over again. "Damn I ain't never seen no pussy lips hang down like this." He slowly worked his dick head in this tight pussy. Wrapped his arms around my waist. We both began to moan and scream. "Damn this pussy feel so good in the inside." I started clapping my ass cheeks on his dick. The more I bounced the louder he get. "Oh shit that's it baby bounce up and down on this dick." He started slapping me on my ass cheeks, pulling my hair kissing me all down my back. He was fucking me so hard cum was dripping down my thighs. Ooh Antonio that's it baby fuck me come on get this pussy faster baby come on! "Oh Shekela I'm bout to nut. Ooh Shekela." After we both nutted so hard we just fell back on the couch breathing sweating like hell. "Damn woman I got one question for you." What's that? "Who taught you how to fuck and suck a dick like that." I started laughing. No one taught me anything I learned myself. I got skills huh. "You damn show do you got my head all fucked up over here. I will love to spend the rest of the morning with you but I got to get up and get to the house before the kids wake up." Trust me I understand. He got up start putting his clothes on. I walked him to the door. "I hate to fucking leave but I gotta go. I got a big day ahead of me, I gotta pick up my mom from the airport she going to come spend the two weeks with me until my wife get here. But I do want to see you later on." Well you got my number I'm just next door call me. He kiss me and hugged me goodbye.

After he left I went upstairs and took a hot bubble bath. Thinking about everything that just happened between me and Antonio. He has no idea what I have in store for him. The wife may be coming here in two weeks but that still give me two weeks to fuck his head up. After I finished I went downstairs and cooked me some breakfast and got in the bed. I called Kiera and woke her up. Girl before I tell you what happened click over and call Alexandria so I can tell you guys together what happened between me and my neighbor. "Don't tell me Shekela you already got that." Girl call Alexandria. She click over and called Alexandria we was all on the phone. Well let me tell you all about the news I fucked Antonio head up this morning. Kiera said "Damn you already got the dick." After y'all drop me off I went upstairs open the blinds and got naked and he watched me play with my nipples and pussy and it was on from there. Alexandria said "You mean to tell me you broke him down in one day." You know me when I'm on a mission I get the job done. We started laughing. Kiera said "Damn Alexandria I wanna be like Shekela." Now you know there is only one Shekela when he made this one there is no other. Alexandria said "Now what's gone happen now you guys done slept together." Honestly we just getting started because he wants to come over tonight. "Are you going to fuck him tonight?" You damn Skippy I am I got two weeks to rock his world before the wife gets here. Well I'm gone talk to you girls later I think I'm gone get a couple of hours of sleep. After we hung up I turned over grabbed a pillow and I went to sleep.

It was about one o'clock I'm just waking up. I heard a whole lot of noise outside. I got up and looked out the window I saw his kids running around playing. I walked over to the night stand and grabbed my cellphone. I started going through my messages. Antonio sent me a message. "This morning was off the hook I can't stop thinking about you. Hope you having a good day." I smiled. I don't think I'm going to text back. Since I got the dick now I'm gone play hard to get. I went into my closet found something to put on. I got dressed and went next door. I rung the door bell he opened up. "Well how are you doing?" I'm doing good I just came over to see if you needed any help. "Dressed like that." What's wrong with what I got on. "Ummm

Shekela if you was coming to help me you wouldn't have a little short mini skirt on, stilettos, and a see through top." Well do I have to go home and change. "You don't have to I'm bout to get ready and leave anyways." OK I don't want to hold you up. "No that's not it remember I told you I got to go to the airport and pick up my mom." Aw you did tell me that I'm sorry. Well I'm gone go let you go and I'm going to go over my sister house and see what she doing. "Well are you going to be at home later." Maybe why? "I may want to come over to see you." We will see you have a good day. "Shekela you behave yourself." I'm always a good girl. "Yeah right." As I was walking away I drop my keys I looked at him I bent over and pick them up I knew he was gone look and smile because I didn't have on any underwear. "You a bad girl." I know and you a bad boy.

I got in my truck and drove off.

"Daddy who is that pretty lady?" She is our next door neighbor lets get in the car kids we can go to the airport and pick up your grandmother.

When I got to my sister house I went inside had a seat. "Tekela girl I think you may want to have a seat. "What's wrong?" Nothing is wrong but me and Antonio got our freak on. "You lying!" Do I lie to you? "No you don't I don't know why I said that. What happen." Girl me Kiera and Alexandria went out last night and when we came back from the club they drop me off and you know me I love attention. I opened up the blinds stood in front of the window and got naked and he watched me. "Oh my God I can't believe you did that." I did and girl I stayed in that window teasing him he got so turned on by it. He came over and we got our fuck on. "I knew it was a matter of time that you was gone fuck him because I know my sister. I got one question for you." What's that? "Was it good?" Yes it was he definitely know how to take care of business and when it come to eating pussy he got it down pack to the Tee. "Now since you fucked him what's next?" Fuck him again again and again. "What you gone do when the wife come?" Like I'm gone let that stop me from getting the dick. "I know you're not gone let that stop you but do you think he's gone play when the wife gets there." If he don't come next door we damn show can go somewhere else and play. "This was just a game to you. You won so why not just move on to some one else." That's what I normally do but it's something about the doctor I like. "We'll just keep one thing in mind." What's that? "He do have a wife and that can become a problem to you." Well you know me I will fix a problem in a minute to make myself happy. "You're my sister Shekela and I don't want to see you hurt. I'm gone be OK I just stop by to tell you what happen.

As I was walking out the door Tekela came behind me "Shekela what are we going to do for our birthday next Saturday lets get together and have a party and invite some friends." Well that sounds good. "When are you gone have time to get the details together since you so wrapped up in the doctor." I smiled at her we will talk about that tomorrow and get all the details together OK.

After I left my sister I headed to the mall to do a lil shopping to get something sexy, smell good for Antonio. My phone rung it was Kiera. "What are you doing?" On my way to the mall. "Well come by and pick me up I want to stop and get a couple of things." OK I'll be there in bout ten minutes. Went by and got her and went to the mall. "I can't believe my girl Shekela done turned the doctor out already. Girl please you know how I get down and dirty. Kiera what are you going to the mall for? "Girl you ain't the only somebody who getting their freak on. I got a hot date tonight." With who? "Robert and when I tell you he is a freak, a brother like to suck toes, eat pussy, lick ass, suck on fingers he do it all girl friend." Damn! Where you meet him at? "At the club about an month ago we been hanging out every since." So tonight he is coming to my house so I want to get some toys and something sexy." Well we going to the same place cause I'm going to get something sexy for Antonio. "Damn Shekela." What? "You always get the good ones I want to be just like you." I started laughing girl you crazy. "No seriously you always get the doctor, Lawyers, the Judges. What the hell you be doing to these men." I can't tell you my secret. "I don't know what you be doing to them but whatever it is you be fucking their heads up. I'm glad I'm not a man I would have to kill you." We started laughing.

When we walked into the mall we went into this exotic store called "Passions Play House" they had everything you could think of sex toys, lingerie, candles, hot oil. Me and Kiera got the hookup. I brought a pair of red boots that come all the way up to my pussy clique. Some sexy lingerie that go with it and a cow boy hat because tonight when I see Antonio I plan on riding that dick like a cowgirl. I bought me a dildo a long black one bout ten in a half inches. I want him to watch me fuck myself.

After we left the mall we went to the grocery store I went one way Kiera went another way. I grabbed some bananas, cucumbers, lolli pops, kit kat bars, twix, eagle brand milk, caramel, hot chocolate. When I got finished I headed to the counter Kiera looked at me "Damn Shekela what is all this for?" Tonight. "Do you use all this stuff in the bedroom?" I sure do. "So tell me what you do with the banana and cucumber." Dip it in some hot chocolate and put it in my pussy and fuck myself with it. "Damn let me go get some of this stuff." When she came back to the counter she looked at me with a smile on her face. She said "Shekela I'm gone have to talk to you about some of the stuff you use for the bedroom. Even though I'm a freak as well I never heard of this stuff before. Where did you learn this stuff from?" I have my own imagination girlfriend. "You sure in the hell do, we got to have a talk." After we left the store all I could do was look at her and laugh. I can't believe you never heard about the banana, the cucumber, the lolli pop, and kit kat bar. "No!" You're late. "Well evidently I must be. So this is what you use to drive them men crazy?" Yes and a whole lot more. "You gone school me on some shit. Wait till I tell Alexandria bout your freaky ass." You come on get your ass in the truck so I can take you home and drop you off, because I got some errands to run. "What you got to go do?" Get my hair, nails, and toes done. "Damn you going all out for Antonio tonight." I want to look good, smell good, taste good, for him. I plan on turning his ass out tonight. "All I can say I wish I was a fly on the wall to see what the hell going on in your bedroom." No you don't "Why you say that?" Trust and believe me I don't want you to hear the man holla like a lil bitch. "Damn it's like that?" Only if you knew. You know next Saturday is our birthday. Yeah I know it's you and Tekela birthday what y'all gone do?" We gone get together and have a party. We haven't got all the details together but be ready to pitch in and help. You know I got y'all back.

After I drop Kiera off I headed to the beauty shop and got hooked up. When I finally made it home Antonio was outside barbecuing. I got out the truck start grabbing my bags. "Well don't you look beautiful." Thank you. "You been gone all day." I had some things I had to take care of. As we were talking his mom came outside. "Mom this is our neighbor Shekela. Shekela this is my mom Mrs. Jackson." "Well how are you Shekela?" I'm doing good how are you Mrs. Jackson? "I'm doing good." Well it was a pleasure meeting you and I hope you guys enjoy y'all barbecue. I walked away went into the house started putting everything up. My phone rung it was my sister. "Kiera told me about the freaky stuff y'all bought." We started laughing. So y'all gone get y'all freak on tonight. That's the plan what about you. "I think I may go out to a movie, I really don't have any plans." Well it sound like to me you should get your freak on. "I got to find a man first." So what are you waiting on. "I got my eye on someone just taking it slow." Well don't be to slow.

So that's your new neighbor, yes that's her she good people but son you know I don't never get in your business. "Mom what you hitting around to?" She's a very attractive woman "Yes she is" don't you go there "What you mean don't go there?" Don't you touch that. I know women like her she looks like she's trouble. "She's not she is an very intelligent woman she's a nurse and we're going to be working at the same hospital together." Aw hell the only thing I'm saying son women like her use what they got to get what they want and I was looking at her the way she was watching you. "You reading to much in to this" Don't tell me that I'm a woman I know these things and I know how women love a challenge. I know about the lil mind games we play. You be careful with her. "We are just friends and neighbors there is nothing going on." Remember what your mama told you don't touch that you have a wife, a family, and a career to think about. "Everything going to be OK mom you always worry."

After I finish talking to my sister I went to the kitchen to get something to eat, the door bell rung when I opened the door it was my homeboy Chris I haven't seen him in a while we started hugging Antonio was looking. He came in and I closed the door we went into the kitchen sat down. He said "Whats going on with you pretty girl I haven't seen you in a while." I been busy, so whats been going on in your world working hard and trying to make this money where is your other half I just got off the phone with her. You know our birthday is next Saturday. "Yeah that's why I stop by to see what y'all was gone do." We're going to have a party but we haven't got everything together yet and you know you on the list. "I see you have a new neighbor." Yes he just moved in yesterday his name is Antonio. "Well you know I'm finna ask you this question here. Have you fucked him yet?" Why would you think that about me? "I don't think you a hoe but I know you. I know what kind of games you like to play remember what happened a couple of years ago with the guy next door? All the bullshit and drama you went through, by the way is he married with kids?" Yes he is. "ALL HELL NO! Don't put yourself through that again it almost caused you your life you're smarter than that don't make the same mistakes again." I'm a big girl I can take care of myself. "I know you are I'm just looking out for you cause I love you, but you still have not answered the question. Have you fucked him yet?" Do you think I fucked him? "Knowing you HELL TO THE YEAH!" To ease your mind no I have not. "I know you a grown ass woman and got a mind of your own, but don't do that to yourself again. You deserve so much better more than that. Try being first for a change instead of second or third. You are a very beautiful woman and you can have any man you want. Don't sale yourself short all the time." I appreciate you looking out for me, but I'm OK I'm gone be OK. Well I got somethings I need to go take care of and I am gone holla at you later." Well let me walk you outside to your car. When I walked Chris outside Antonio was standing in the door looking at me. "I see your neighbor watching you." Bye Chris. "Don't play with me Shekela come give me a hug before I go." When Chris drove off Antonio came outside. We looked at each other. Antonio said "We got plenty of Barbecue you want some?" Sure why not. "I'ma go fix you a plate I'll be right back." When he came out and gave me the food. "That must be your boyfriend?" No he is not, he is my best friend. "Are you fucking him?" No! Are you jealous? "Should I be?" No you shouldn't like I said he's my best friend. "What you finna do?" Go in the house and eat this food you just gave me. "Well let me go back inside and finish cooking." Well thank you for the plate. As I was walking away "Shekela" I turned around "I'ma call you later." OK I'll talk to you later. I walked in the house went to the living room sat down and start eating. The food was good all I could think about was him.

So you not listening to your at all mother huh? "What are you talking about?" I see you outside talking to your neighbor fixing her a plate. "That's the least I could do mom we are neighbors." Son you are a grown man I'm not going to say anything else anymore, but don't say I didn't tell you so. She walked away I went into the kitchen and finished cooking. But the only thing was on my mind is how good she can fuck and suck a dick. Ian never had pussy that good in my life. DAMN! I hope I don't have to pay the price for it in the end, but it's hard like hell to stay away from this woman right now.

After I finished eating, I laid on the couch and dozed off. As I was waking up the phone rung it was Antonio. "What are you doing beautiful?" I'm just waking up. "What are you gone be doing about nine o'clock?" I don't know. What do you have in mind? "I'm going to tell my mother I'm going out for a while I'm take my car around the corner and park it, and I'm come back to your house." You sure you want to do that? "Don't you want to see me?" Yes I do, but do you want to take that risk of leaving. You don't think your mother would get suspicious. "About what I'm grown ass man." Yeah you are but you're also a married man. "You didn't think about my wife last night when you was fucking my brains out." Is that what I did to you? "You know you fucked me up last night that's why I'm coming back." So what are you trying to say if I wasn't good you wouldn't came back? "Honestly No." Well at least you are keeping it real. So tell me something Antonio. "What's that?" What's gone happen between us when your wife get here? "I don't know, but I can tell you one thing she don't fuck and suck my dick like you." Well I guess I will see you at nine o'clock. "OK beautiful." After we hung up I got up and started cleaning up. I took me a hot bubble bath lit some candles all over the house, put on some soft music put some champagne on ice and took everything I needed to the bedroom. My phone rung it was Kiera and Alexandria. "Well we know what you finna do tonight." Yes I'm finna get my freak on and I do not have time to talk to you girls right about now. "All so its like that you don't have time for us right now." Well Kiera don't you have some dick to get tonight? "He don't get off until ten." Well my dick coming over at nine so I got somethings I got to do. So I'll talk to you girls tomorrow. After I finished setting the mood getting everything together. I went into my bedroom and started getting ready. I look so good right now it's gone make his heart skip a beat. I got these red boots on that come up to my pussy these booty shorts with all this ass everywhere matching bra. Damn I'm fine as hell, but that's the wrong thing he should have told me bout the wife she can't fuck him good or suck his dick. Come on ladies now you know I gotta take advantage of that shit there. She cant twerk this ass on him like me. When I get through with him he ain't gone be able to keep his dick out this pussy. That I promise you because I know me and what I'm capable of doing.

Chapter 2

My phone rung. Hello. "I'm at your back door." I'll be right there. I walked my sexy ass downstairs opened the back door. "Got damn!" Well come on in. So you like what you see? "Damn girl!" Wait until you see the back I slowly turned around. "Girl you got ass on you for days! I like it thick and don't nothing turn me on more than a red ass woman with a lot of ass." Well I got it from my mama. He smiled, he walked up to me place his tongue in my mouth we started tongue kissing he was rubbing that ass with both his hands. "Damn you smell good and I know you taste good." Come with me I got a surprise for you. I grabbed him by the hand and lead him upstairs to my bedroom. "Damn this is nice." I want you to have a seat right here in this recliner chair I want you to watch me entertain you. Let me fix you a drink. I turn on some soft music, he laid back. Are you afraid of being handcuffed? He smiled "I don't know I never been handcuff before." Well tonight you will be don't panic I'm not gone hurt you I'm just gone make you feel good like hell. I put the handcuffs on him I started dancing in front of him I slowly turned around and put my ass all in his face. He started kissing me on my ass cheeks. I sat on his lap I can feel his dick jumping all around my pussy. "Damn you smell so good." I got up and got the whip cream. I took off my bra and threw it in his face. I poured whip cream all over my nipples and started to suck and lick on them. I skeet hot chocolate all over my tongue walked up to him and place it in his mouth. We started kissing. I sat on the edge of the bed and spread my legs wide open took the banana poured hot chocolate all over it. I laid back in the bed and put my legs over my head and place that banana in and out my wet juicy tight pussy. I started moaning. "Shekela I can't take this shit no more. You got to un handcuff me so I can stick my tongue in that wet pussy." No baby its not time yet just watch me stick this banana in and out my pussy. I was fucking myself so hard with that banana the cum was dripping between my ass cheeks I took my finger and place it inside my ass hole I started fucking myself as I continue to play with my pussy with the banana he was moaning calling my name telling me to please un handcuff me baby come on I can't take this" It's not time yet baby. "Fuck that un handcuff me and let me eat that pussy come on." All I could do is look at him and smiled. Antonio it is not time yet sweetie. "What the hell you mean its not time yet I can't take this shit my dick is so hard it can crack a window." Give me another five minutes and I will un handcuff you. I got up walked over to the night stand open it up and pulled out my Ten in a half inch dildo. "What the hell is that for?" Just watch keep your eyes on me. I placed the dildo on the floor and I squat down pushed my pussy lips up and down on it while I was playing with my nipples. "Damn Shekela a brother can't take no more of this shit." I started bouncing up and down moaning calling his name Antonio! I looked into his eyes did you want to fuck me? "Hell yeah!" After I got off the dildo I looked down at it. It had thick white cum all over it. I picked it up stood in front of Antonio and lick the cum off that dildo. "You nasty ass freak take these handcuffs off me so I can fuck the shit outta you!" After I cut him loose his cellphone rung. He looked at it "Damn Shit!" What is it? "My wife I got to answer this!" As he pick it up I hurried up took his dick out and started sucking on it. "Hey sweetie" Hey baby how you doing? "I'm doing OK." I called the house the kids said you wasn't there. "I'm at the hospital talking to one of the doctors that we're working with Monday but baby I got to call you back cause I'm talking right now." OK. "Damn Shekela you almost made me scream your name girl!" He started pushing my head up and down on his dick. I can feel the hot cum dripping all down my chin. "Oh baby don't stop shit suck my dick like you was sucking that dildo." He took his hand wrapped it around the back of my hair pushed my head farther down. I can feel his dick head hit the back of my throat as I'm swallowing his cum down like water. He was hollering and screaming my name so loud I was hoping no one outside heard him. I raised up he took his tongue started licking the cream off my face. "Damn baby no woman has ever made me holler like that before when I say you got skills girl you got skills." He pick me up laid me across the bed he pulled my thong off I want to fuck you with your boots on he reached over to the night stand and grabbed a condom. He started sucking on my nipples licking me all down my stomach spread them legs apart sucking on that pussy. I started moaning that's it baby eat that pussy aw shit. He took his tongue spread my ass cheeks apart sliding his tongue between the crack of my ass cheeks. Aw this shit feels so good he was going to the ass to the pussy to the pussy to the ass just licking and kissing it all on it damn all baby shit. He pushed his dick inside of my tight pussy and started fucking me. We both were moaning like hell. "Aw Shit oh-we damn Shekela damn baby this pussy good. Look at all the cum on my dick from your pussy." I started sucking on my nipples aw baby shit. He started pushing that dick deeper into my pussy and that's when all hell broke loose. We started fucking the shit out of each other. Breathing all hard ooh baby fuck me that's it fuck me. His phone rung again I looked at him. Do you want stop and answer that? "Hell to the no all I want you to do is fuck me throw that pussy on this dick oh-we come on Shekela fuck me baby come on that's it baby fuck me." I started fucking the shit outta him. I took my hand and place it over his mouth because I didn't want my neighbors to hear him call my name. That pussy was so good to him he bit my finger. "Come on baby girl turn this ass over so I can hit this shit from the back." I turned over and put this ass in the air for him. He was slapping them ass cheeks as he was pushing his dick in and out this pussy. My ass cheeks was slapping on his dick, I can feel his balls just bouncing up and down hitting my ass cheeks. I was fucking his ass so good he started biting me all on my neck and back pushing his finger in my ass hole. "Oh Shekela oh baby oh Shekela I'm finna nut baby I'm finna nut!" Come on baby come on do your shit come on fuck me! "Oh baby here it comes come on baby lets nut together come on baby." "Ooh Shekela, ooh girl what are you doing to me?" Making you feel like you are the man. After he got that long as nut he laid beside me with a big smile on his face. "Damn girl what am I going to do with you?" Continue to fuck me like you just did and we gone get along just fine. "All I got is one thing to say when a man is fucking you he may want to start taking Viagra cause your ass will wear a man dick out." You don't need no Viagra all you need is me cause I damn show can keep that dick up and going. "Well you don't gotta tell me I know what you can do. You will kill a man." I'm not trying to kill nobody I just want them to know this pussy is the bomb. "Let me ask you a question?" What's that? "The guy who was at your house today are you fucking him?" No I'm not. "The way he hug you, you will think y'all was fucking." He's like my big brother. "You mean to tell me he ain't never tried to get the pussy?" Of course he did I just didn't see him that way and I will never want to do anything to mess up our friendship. He raised up and got his cellphone. "Damn it's almost Twelve o'clock I got to get my ass up and get to the house. Would it be OK if I took a shower?" Aw that will be the smart thing to do you don't want to go home smelling like sex. He started laughing "Are you going to take one with me?" No I will wait until you get through. "Why?" Because if I get in the shower with you we gone end up fucking all over again and I know you got to go home. "Your right because if you take another shower with me I won't be going home tonight." I looked at him he got up and went took a shower. I laid across the bed thinking to myself. I hope this shit don't backfire on me I'm not trying to get hurt I'm trying to do the hurting but if he keeps fucking me like that I'ma fuck around and get hooked on his dick and that is not gone be a good thing because he is married. Maybe I should step back a lil bit and do me focus my mind on something else besides him, but its gone be hard as hell to do that when the dick and the tongue good as hell. When he came out the shower he started getting dress he sat next to me. "I like you a lot I didn't have any idea when I moved right next door to you this would be going on." Do you have any regrets? "No I don't. What about you? "No, Shekela look at me I don't want us to stop being friends." What make you think we are? "I don't know but I don't want that to happen and it's not just the pussy talking this is me talking from the heart, I like you." Well I like you too. "I think you are an amazing woman every man fantasy you do shit to me that my wife wouldn't even think about doing you got me all messed up in the head, but I do want to know one thing are you fucking anybody besides me?" Once again no I'm not. "This may sound selfish as hell and I may be wrong to ask you this but please don't fuck nobody else besides me." You right you are being selfish. "I'm being serious right now." How could you ask me that and your wife will be here in two weeks then what? "We will deal with that when she get here right now I want you all to myself." That's just the pussy talking. "No it's not I don't want to share you with no one." What I suppose to do be lonely and fuck you when you can fuck me. "I'm gone do everything I can to try to spend time with you remember we work together I will see you everyday." OK outside the job I may want to see you on my time and you can't see me what do I suppose to do come home and play with my pussy by myself? "I know it's asking a whole lot and I am being selfish right now I just don't want to share you." Antonio lets just play it by ear and see what happens. "OK I have to accept that. Are you going to walk me to the door?" Yes. When we made it to the door he just look at me. "I had a real good time tonight and this is a night I will never forget. You made me feel like I never felt before." I had fun too. "I'm go home and call my wife, and later on tonight I'ma call you and we gone talk alright." That's fine. He hugged me and kiss me good night. After he left I went back upstairs started cleaning up my room took me a bath went into the kitchen and fixed me a snack laid on the couch and watch TV, thinking about everything he just said what am I going to do. Is this a game to me? Am I going to allow myself to get serious with this man or do I need to see other people to keep my mind focused because I'm not going to let Antonio hurt me.

About forty five minutes later my phone rung it was him calling to say good night. Did you talk to your wife. "We talked but I couldn't go to bed without talking to you." Well that's very sweet of you. "So what are you doing now?" Laying down on the couch watching TV I think I'm go to bed too I'm tired. He started to laugh. What's funny? "I'm tired as hell myself you wore my ass out." Well you should sleep like a baby tonight. "Trust me I am, well you gone go to bed beautiful I will talk to you tomorrow." OK you have a good night. "You too."

After we hung up I went upstairs and got in the bed I dozed off and went to sleep. It was about five thirty in the morning I heard the phone ringing I looked at the phone it was Antonio. I was tempted to answer I don't want him to think I'm gone be available every time he call me. I can't do that to myself. He left me a voice mail. "I was hoping you would be up I really wanted to talk to you but I do understand you got to get your beauty sleep as well. I can't stop thinking about you Shekela. I will talk to you later alright." I am not going to allow myself to get caught up in his world and I get hurt. I got to get out and see other people now.

It was about Ten o'clock Sunday morning I got up got dressed and headed out. I went to Kiera house to talk to her about what's going on with me and Antonio. When I got there she was cooking breakfast. "Well how was your date with Antonio last night?" It was all good what about your date? "It was off the hook!" I want talk to you about something. "Awl hell, what the doctor then did now?" He haven't done anything yet. "What do you mean yet?" You know this was a game to me. "OK." Me personally I think he letting his feelings get involved and that's not what I want because he is married. This was just a game and a challenge for me. "So Shekela, wait let me understand this you fucking the man brains out and you think he ain't gone catch feelings for you. Do you like him?" Yes that's the problem, I do like him but I know he has a wife. "Well you never let that stop you before." But there is a difference now I didn't care anything about those other guys, it was a game then just like it is now but my feelings are getting involved as well and I can't let that happened. "What are you going to do now?" I don't know I'm just thinking about seeing other people, because he don't want me sleeping with nobody but him. "Well are you going to do that?" I don't know. Chris came by yesterday and he did remind me about what happen two years ago with my other neighbor I got involved with. "You know Shekela I didn't want to say anything or bring it up to you but you do need to think about what happen. Antonio seems like a nice guy but you're right he got a wife and kids, you don't want to go down that road again the fuck may be good but is it worth your life. You're 25 years old now, you need to settle down and get you a man and be happy. Because you're not gone be happy when you got somebody else man especially a married man, ain't nothing but drama and problems gone come." But I do like him. "I know you do because he is fine as hell. Hell I even looked at him. Well you're a grown ass woman, I can't tell you what to do but you think about everything. Do you want to be the other woman? Or do you want the be the woman? You can walk away from this because it started off as a game and you won you done slept with him now." You're right but damn girl that man got some good dick and a fye ass tongue. We started laughing. "Is it worth your life though because if he can't let you go you gone have a bigger problem on your hand. The wife then on top of all that you guys gone be working together seeing each other everyday." If Chris ask you am I fucking Antonio say no. "Well to be honest this ain't got a damn thing to do with Chris." I know it don't but he's like my big brother, and he is concerned about me just like you are. "Girl Chris might be concerned but he been trying to fuck you for the longest his ass just mad cause he ain't got the pussy yet and he should be glad he ain't got it, because the way these guys act when you fuck them they need counseling behind this shit." She started laughing. "But I tell you one thing Shekela see when his wife make it here see how much time he gone give you then. But then again I don't know when you fuck them they just get stupid in the head." All I could do was look at Kiera, girl you crazy.

"What y'all gone do for y'all birthday Saturday." I don't know come to think about it let me call her and tell her to come over here and we can get some stuff together. I reached in my purse and grabbed my phone and called my sister. I'm over Kiera house you ain't doing nothing which I know you probably ain't come over here we can get the birthday stuff together. "I'll be there in about thirty minutes."

"Are you going to invite Antonio to the party?" I don't think so. "Why not?" Why should I? "You gone be alone on your birthday with no dick." I didn't say all that now. "Girl you fuck around and give that pussy to somebody else Antonio gone act a fool." I'm not Antonio wife, I'm not even his girlfriend. We are just bed friends. "OK sure you're right."

When my sister made it over here we gathered around the kitchen table eating, laughing and talking. "So how was y'all date last night?" Kiera said "Well maybe you should ask your sister, I think hers was better than mine." She looked at me. "So how was it with the doctor last night?" It was good we had a good time. "But you left out one lil small part." What's that? "You forgot to tell her, he maybe pussy whip already." "Damn Shekela what you do to him?" "You know what your sister did to that man don't act crazy. Your sister like the doctor. "Nawl tell me it ain't so. Shekela you like Antonio?" I like the way Antonio fucks me. Kiera started laughing. "How in the hell do a player let her feelings get involved?" If you was player like your sister you would know these things. Even players have feelings. "Well I hope you don't let your feelings get the best of you." Can we talk about the birthday party? "The birthday party can wait. You must forgot about what happened to you a couple of years ago?" If one more person bring that shit up I'm gone holler. "Well you better think about because this is not a game anymore if his feelings got involved, your feelings got involved somebody is bound to get hurt." "Shekela you know your sister is right. Somebody always get hurt when you messing around with the married man." Kiera also said "What you should have done is fucked him that one time and didn't go back no more and move to the next one. But nawl you had to go back a second time." When you get some good dick its hard to stay away from it. My sister said "Ain't no dick worth my life, I don't give a damn how good it is." Well when you get some good dick sister, I guarantee you it will make you think twice its hard to find some good dick. "You right about that it is hard to find some but some good dick will get you caught up." Hell if you get some bad dick it will get you caught up. "Nawl bad dick don't get you caught up cause you ain't going back to the bad shit, but you will act a fool over some good shit." Kiera said "Wait a minute I got an ideal. Why don't y'all have y'all birthday party at my house?" "That's a good idea but Shekela are you going to tell Antonio about the party." "Damn that's the same thing I asked her." No I'm not. "You might as well tell him y'all fucking." Look sister get you some business and stay out of mine. "OK mama always said hard head makes an soft ass, you got hurt messing around with a married and got out of that. This time you might not be so lucky that's all I'm saying. I appreciate you guy worrying bout me I really do I know what I'm doing. Yes I admit I like him. I admit I like him but damn it wasn't suppose to happen that way it suppose to been a fuck and move on. Kiera said "Shekela let me tell you something you should have been born a man and don't get offended about that and let me tell you why I say that. You know when a man go to a car dealership and they have to test drive about three or four cars before they figure out which one they are going to buy. That's how you are when It comes to a dick. You got to fuck two or three guys to figure out which one the dicks are the best that suits you. But see obviously you been getting some dick but ain't nan one of them dicks got you on lock down. Now Antonio moved next door to you and looked what happened you thought you was gone play the little game with him and fuck him and move on but your feelings got involved now you don't know what to do about it. But let me tell you something about a year ago I was fucking this guy girl I thought I was love with him but in three weeks I found out otherwise. I didn't love him hell I didn't even care about the man I just like the way he fuck me and ate my pussy and after that was over I moved on to the next one. Don't get it twisted I'm not saying this was going on between you and Antonio you might do like him and start caring about him but one thing about it he got a wife and that's going to become a problem, but you can find out if he just like you or the pussy you a woman you know what to do. I can tell you one thing baby girl if he like you every time he see you he not gone want to fuck you he gone want to spend sometime with you, get to know everything about Shekela not what Shekela got between her legs. For one thing his wife may not be fucking him like you." He told me she didn't. "See there a typical man will another woman his wife ain't doing her duties. But one thing about a man when he get some good pussy it's hard to let that shit go. Just like Shekela, he done told you his wife ain't doing the shit like you. See you putting the shit on his ass. If the shit was bad girl he wouldn't even call you the next day. But you know what we just like them if we get some bad dick we ain't gone fuck it no more but, if we get some good dick girl we will hound that shit down like a wet dog. But we all done had our share on good and bad. Shekela done got her a good one look at her." My sister just looked at me. "I wonder how he gone act when the wife get there." Well I will just deal with that when it happens, but right now I'm just gone get the dick. My sister said "Do you know anything about his wife?" No and I'm not trying to know anything about her. "Well I think you should at least have the upper hand on her." Kiera said "I agree with your sister. Never let the wife know more about you then you know about her. Remember Shekela you are the other woman and you need to be on point especially when she gets there, because she gone look at you probably talk about you to him. He ain't gone say nothing he ain't gone talk about you. You know why because he fucking you. And if she's just an average looking woman she gone be on point about her husband. I know I would be. Ain't no way in the hell I would have let him come to Atlanta for two weeks and I didn't come with him she must don't want her husband. Evidently she don't know the ATL women we will snatch they ass up in a minute. You could look at a brother and tells he works out. Shekela I don't blame you get that dick." We all started laughing.

A few moments later my cellphone rung I looked at it. Speaking of the devil. Kiera said "Don't answer let him leave a message. Never let your self be available for him every time he call you." Damn Kiera we thing alike. "Now call your cell phone put it on speaker and let us hear that voice mail he left you." Let's see what he got to say. "Hey Shekela this Antonio I can see you not at home you must be out and about, but I'm just waking up. I woke up with you on my mind, I can't stop thinking about last night. I had an amazing time with you. You are an amazing woman as well. You might not believe this but I want to get to know everything about you. I don't want you to think that this is all about sex, I want to get to know you. So call me when you get a chance. If I don't pick up leave a message, or I will just talk to you when you get home. Have a good day beautiful aite." We all just looked at each other. Kiera said "Maybe it's not all about the pussy maybe he really do like you." My sister said "Still Shekela be careful cause at the end of the day he do have a wife baby girl." OK I understand he got a wife, he's not the only married man that cheats. "Well you should know better than all of us, because some reason you attracts married men. I like fucking around with married men because it's a challenge to me, because woman well let me say some women thinks because a man got a ring on his finger he won't cheat. That's bullshit hell even married women cheats. You know how we women are sometimes we want things we can't have but do we let that stop us. No we don't. Kiera reply "Since we got that out the way let's cook a Sunday dinner at my house. We definitely need to go to the store. And one of y'all call Alexandria and tell her we having dinner here." We got up and headed to the grocery store started to get everything we gone cook. We got back to Kiera house started to get everything together. We made some drinks put on some music and we started having a party. Alexandria showed up. Everything was ready. We sat the dinner table, we gathered around bow our heads and we prayed. When we finished we sat down. We started talking. Alexandria said "I got a problem y'all and I know y'all can help me." What's that? "This guy I'm talking to." Kiera said "Awl hell." She said "What?" "You should have been here earlier. We talked about Shekela and the doctor all morning." "Aw yeah that's right I heard about your night with him last night. How did that go?" It was good. Now back to your problem. "Y'all know I been creeping around with Keshun for about eight months. Did I tell y'all he got engaged to his girlfriend?" No you didn't tell us that. "Well I didn't find out until yesterday he told me he proposed to her." Um how you feel about that? "I'm kind of pissed off about it cause this morning I took a home pregnancy test and found out I'm pregnant." Kiera said "Damn have you told him?" "I tried to call him this morning he didn't pick up." My sister said "Y'all gone leave these women men alone ain't nothing but problems behind that shit." Are you replying to me? "No I'm not I'm just saying. Get your own men and you won't have to worry about these problems." Well I disagree with you sister. You can have a man and still have problems how you know he ain't out cheating on you. "That might be so but at least I can say that's my man and not somebody else." When you get through talking we all sharing the same dick. We might not know about it but we are. So Alexandria what you gone do? "I'm gone tell him I'm pregnant either he gone do it the right way or I'm gone give his ass hell about it." Well it ain't too much hell you can give him because you knew he had a woman. Alexandria looked at Tekela "You mean to tell me you don't think your man fucking on you." "I didn't say that I'm not saying he won't cheat. But at least I can pick up the phone and go to him when I get ready." "Well that might be true but he is still a man. Don't think for one minute he won't stick his dick in some pussy cause he will. Because if the opportunity knocked at the door being a man he will fucking take it." "Well that's where you wrong Alexandria cause all men are not hoes." "I didn't say they all was hoes but ninety percent of them are hoes." Well that's your opinion. My opinion is this a man only do what a woman allow him to do. Kiera said "Well she right about that y'all." One thing about we women when we with a man and we love and care about him we will put up with some bull shit for a while. But eventually we will get tired of it. Some of will wake up and smile the coffee some of us won't. Some women are in denial about their man fucking off on them, just to say they have a man to come home and pay the bills for them. Well I'm not looking for a man to take of me I can take care myself I work five days a week. "Well Tekela a lot of women is not that fortunate to have a career." They can have a career if that's something they want. It's no such thing as can't have a career. Alexandria asked me "Since you sleeping with Antonio and you know he is married do you think he will fuck another woman on you?" I don't know and if he do that's not my problem because I'm not the wife. "Well I'll be pissed off you the other woman." That's what y'all fell to understand I'm not his other woman. I'm just his next door neighbor and we fucking. "Come on Shekela it's more than just sex, you like the man." That might be true, but I'm not gone ask him to leave his wife for me. He will turn around and leave me for someone else. My sister said "Well when you cheating with someone else man that don't belong to you, and when you get one and when he cheat on you. You can't get mad, because you doing the same thing. Fucking somebody else man that don't belong to you. You know what Shekela I don't think you want a relationship with anybody cause you know what you done." What you trying to say? "Just about every man you done been with was with somebody. Think about it." If I recall Tekela you slept with a married man before. You done dated somebody who had a woman. "You right I have and in the end I got hurt. But it only made me smarter to get my own man and not somebody else." Alexandria said "Well you know what I'm not mad at Shekela." Tekela said "I'm not mad at my sister neither she's a grown ass woman she can do what she wanna do. I just don't want to see her get hurt because I know she deserves the best." Well I appreciate you looking out for your sister. But I got this and you know what when the wife do get here and we don't fuck again it's all good because if sure as shit stank if I found one good dick I damn sho can find another one probably better. When GOD made one he didn't stop making them. Kiera said "Amen to that. I done had my share of good ones and they are definitely out there. One thing about us women we will find some good dick it may take us a while but we will find some. And one thing about a man when they get some good pussy they not gone let it go too quickly especially if they got a wife or a girlfriend or just a sex partner and it ain't good they going back to the good shit." The only thing I'm saying ladies is this yes I know it's wrong to be fucking him he got a wife, but I didn't put a gun to his head and made him come to my house and fuck me he did that on his own. Yes I played a part in it and let it happen because you know why I wanted it just like he did. And at the end of the day it doesn't matter what none of you guys say I'm still gone fuck Antonio whether you like or not. When I get tired of the bullshit you know what I know how to end it and move the fuck on and get a man of my own but right now I'm having some fun with the doctor case closed. Alexandria said "Well I guess she told our asses off didn't she." Nawl I wasn't trying to tell nobody off I'm just letting y'all know I am gone do me no matter what nobody say. After we finished talking, eating, and laughing. We got up and started cleaning up. It was getting late and we all had to go to work the next day. We all hugged and said our goodbyes.

I headed home so I could get my work clothes together. When I pulled in the driveway Antonio Mom and his two kids was outside. I got out my truck I spoke, she waved back. When I got inside, I headed upstairs and ran me a hot bubble bath. My phone rung I looked at it. It was Antonio.

Me:	Hello.
Him:	Well hey there.
Me:	Hey how you doing?
Him:	Much better now I hear your voice. You been gone all day.

Me:	Yeah I been hanging out with my friends.
Him:	I called you.
Me:	I know.
Him:	You wasn't gone call me back?
Me:	I was gone call you when I made it to the house.
Him:	What are you doing now?
Me:	I'm about to take a hot bubble bath and get my work clothes together.
Him:	Well can I call you back later on tonight.
Me:	Sure.
Him:	Well I'll talk to you later.
Me:	OK.

We hung up.

I went into the bathroom. Looked in the mirror and smiled, thinking to myself that dick is gone belong to me and only me when I get through with him. I took off my clothes and got in the tub. When I finished taking a bath I walked into my bedroom naked drying off. My phone rung. I picked it up.

Antonio:	Are you trying to give me an heart attack.
Me:	What are you talking about.
Antonio:	I'm looking out my bedroom window and I can see you ass naked and you wet as shit.
Me:	Do that bother you?
Antonio:	You know it do.
Me:	Well too bad you can't come and play.
Antonio:	What's stopping me?
Me:	You got to get up early in morning we both do and be at the hospital.
Antonio:	If you know that why you teasing me.
Me:	I'm not honestly I forgot I had the blind opened.
Antonio:	I wish I could come over and grease your body down with my tongue.

I started laughing.

Me: You know you can come over here we both gone be late for work in the morning let me finish drying off and I'm gone call you back.

Antonio: OK sexy.

About forty five minutes later I called him back.

Me: Can you talk

Him: Yes I been waiting on you to call me.

Me: Well I had some stuff I had to do. Where your mom and the kids?

Him: My mom sleep and the kids getting ready for school tomorrow.

Me: How old are the kids?

Him: My daughter is five my son is seven.

Me: It's so much about you I don't know.

Him: Well I'm thirty five you know I got two kids I'm married I'm from Dallas. I been a doctor about five years, been married eight.

Me: Is your wife your high school sweetheart.

Him: No she's not.

Me: Well do you have any brothers or sisters.

Him: I have a brother and two sisters.

Me: So how did you and your wife meet.

Him: At a birthday party.

Me: Is she sexy?

He started laughing.

Me: What's funny?

Him: She's an OK looking woman.

Me: Just OK?

Him: She's the mother of my kids.

Me: That's not what I asked you. Is she sexy?

Him: She's not as sexy as you.

Me:	Well she must be a red woman, because last night you said you love red women.
Him:	She's not red she's brown skin. Now tell me about you.
Me:	Well you know my name is Shekela my last name is Baker I'm twenty five no kids. I'm not in a relationship I haven't been in one in two years.
Him:	And why is that.
Me:	Haven't found the right person.
Him:	As sexy as you are and you having a hard time finding the right man.
Me:	It's not that I'm just picky as hell.
Him:	Well how long you been a nurse.
Me:	Almost four years.
Him:	Where you born and raised in Atlanta.
Me:	Yes I was.
Him:	Have you always been a freak.
Me:	Every since I was sixteen.
Him:	Damn. Well I bet you have broke a lot of men heart.
Me:	You think so.
Him:	I know so the way you been fucking me damn near got my heart already.
Me:	I'm just good at what I do. So what made you move to Atlanta.
Him:	More money.
Me:	If you don't mind me asking what do your wife do for a living?
Him:	She works at a bank.
Me:	Do you love your wife?
Him:	Yes I do.
Me:	Well let me rephrase the question. Are you in love with your wife?
Him:	Not like I use to be.
Me:	What happen.
Him:	Sometimes people just fall out of love.
Me:	So why are you still with her?
Him:	The kids.

Me:	I heard that so many times.
Him:	What?
Me:	Guys say they stay married to the woman because of the kids.
Him:	Well I can't speak for all guys I can only speak for myself.
Me:	Well you don't have to be married to her to take care of your kids.
Him:	I know that. I want to raise my kids with their mom. Is anything wrong with that?
Me:	I guess not you still married to her. Why are you sleeping with me then?
Him:	I'm attracted to you. I like you. I want to get to know you.
Me:	You are a married man.
Him:	I know I'm married and I know I'm wrong, but sometimes married men fuck up.
Me:	Well sometimes married men only fuck up when they are not happy or the sex ain't good. Which one it is to you?
Him:	Both.
Me:	So how many times have you cheated on your wife?
Him:	I'm gone tell you the truth Shekela and you might not believe this but you are the first one. When I was in Dallas I didn't have time to cheat. I was working long hours, spending times with the kids. When I wasn't at work me and her was together all the time.
Me:	One thing about a man though sweetie if he want to play he will find the time to play.
Him:	Your right but I never cheated before until I met you. It's just something about you. Right now you have this effect on me I don't know what to do about it. Today when you was gone all day I couldn't stop thinking about you I wanted to be with you, not just for the sex to see that beautiful smile on your face

	those bedroom eyes. You are a very intriguing woman and that keeps me aroused.
Me:	Well I'm flattered I like you as well. I'm not trying to get hurt.
Him:	I'm not trying to hurt you I just want to get to know you.
Me:	That's all good, but in the back of my mind I'm thinking what's gone happen to us when your wife get here. I know what you told me, but when sex is involved a person will tell you anything to keep getting the sex.
Him:	I understand your word about all that but like I told you I'm not trying to hurt you.
Me:	Well I think we both should say goodnight because we got to get up in the morning.
Him:	To be honest with you I really don't want to hang up but I know I got to. I got to make sure the kids are in the bed and I got to get me a goodnight sleep.
Me:	I know you do. I'll see you at work in the morning.
Him:	I know you will I hope I be able to maintain myself when I see you walking down that hallway tomorrow.
Me:	I'm sure you will, but you gone head and take care the kids. I'm gone get ready to go to sleep.
Him:	OK sexy. See you tomorrow.
Me:	OK you have a good night.

After we hung up I laid there for about twenty minutes thinking could this be possible. Could he actually have feelings for me already. Or it's the pussy talking to him in do time I will know. It's easy said then done when you say you not gone let your feelings get involved but when you start fucking somebody and you are attracted to that person feelings are going to get involved and mine has. I hope and pray that Antonio don't hurt me. If I find out he is playing with my emotions, feelings, and heart he's going to see another side he has never seen before and it won't be anything pretty.

Chapter 3

It's about five in the morning I'm getting up getting my day started. I jumped in the shower did my make up and my hair and got dressed. I went downstairs and had some breakfast. I looked at my watch it was about six thirty. Damn let me get out of here. As I was walking out the door looked up and seen Antonio and his mom. We spoke to each other I got into my truck and headed to work.

Antonio I know you ain't looking at that woman like I think you are. "Mom what are you talking about?" Don't mom me. The way you looked at her and smiled. "You reading to much into this we are neighbors." OK I'm done with this. I done had this talk with you. "You have a good day mom. Make sure when the kids get home from school they don't go outside without doing their homework." He go into his car and headed to work.

When I made it to work I clock in me and my sister was in the hallway talking. "Did you see Antonio last night?" No I didn't I talk to him and I went to bed. "Shekela I don't want you to think I'm dipping in your business it's not that you my sister and I love you and I don't want to see anything happen to you." I understand that and I appreciate all that but everything gone be OK not lets get to work.

It's lunch time and I haven't seen Antonio yet. My sister sent me a text and told me to meet her in the cafeteria for lunch. As we was sitting there my cellphone rung. It was Kiera "Well how is your first day working with the doctor?" I wouldn't know we haven't bump heads yet. "You mean to tell me you ain't seen the doctor yet and y'all find a empty room to get y'all freak on." Bye Kiera.

Our lunch break was over and it was time to get back to work. As I was walking down the hallway I told my sister I would be right back I got to step into the ladies room. "Well I'll wait on you right here."

My sister Tekela was standing in the hallway. Antonio came around the corner. "Damn there go my baby girl right there I haven't seen her all day." He walks up "Hey sexy." Tekela turn around "Excuse me." "I just said hey sexy." "Do I know you?" "What do you mean do you know me." I walked out the bathroom. He looked he took a few steps back "Y'all look just alike." I smiled at him this is my sister Tekela. Tekela this is Antonio my neighbor. "Wow you didn't tell me you had an identical twin sister." You didn't ask me. "Aw man this is funny." What's so funny about it? "I thought she was you and I walked up behind her and said hey sexy. Well Tekela I apologize I thought you was Shekela." "That's OK a lot of people can't tell us apart. But you guys have a good day." When she walked off "I can't believe you didn't tell me you had a twin sister I'm sitting here looking at the both of you and I can't even tell y'all apart." We get that a lot. By the way how was your first day at work. "It's good I was missing you." Well I got to get back to work but I hope you enjoy the rest of your first day. "I want to see you later on tonight." We will see. I walked off. "Damn she fine as hell even in uniform."

It's about three o'clock time for me to get off. After I had finished taking care of everything I had bump into my sister. "Damn Shekela he is fine. I see why you don't want to let that go." I just laughed at her. As we was standing in the hallway talking another doctor name Mr. McGee walked up. "Well hey ladies." Hey Mr. McGee. "How are you ladies doing?" We are doing good now. We all started laughing. "Are you ladies off work?" Yes we are. Moments later Antonio walked up "Have you ladies met the new doctor we have here?" Yes we have he's my next door neighbor. "For real?" Antonio just smiled. My sister cell phone rung. She said "I got to take this but I will talk to all y'all later." Well I got to go too I got some stuff I had to do. I walked off. Mr. McGee said "That's a fine ass woman right there." Antonio just looked at him. "And you're her neighbor?" Yes I am. "You lucky ass man." Why you say that? "If I was living next door to her shidd I don't think I would be able to keep my hands off that. Let me ask you a question Antonio. "Are you married?" Yes I am. "Do your wife look like that?" Antonio just laughed. No I'm not gone lie to you no she don't. "Well you know it's gone be a problem." Why you say that? "If your wife catch you looking at that you think she ain't gone trip." Me and Shekela are just neighbors. "Well I wish I was Shekela next door neighbor. Well Antonio I'm gone holla at you later I got to get back to my rounds." OK. After he walked off Antonio just looked at him. I could see now me and him gone have a problem if he think for one minute I'm gone let him get my goodies.

After I got off of work I went by Alexandria house to see how she was doing about her situation. Have you talked to your baby daddy? "Yes I talked to him." What he had to say? "He mad at me because I stop taking my birth control pills." Why did you stop taking them? "Because they was making me sick." So why come y'all didn't use condoms? "He don't like them." Well he can't be mad at you he can only be mad at his self because he didn't want to wrap his dick up. "He told me if he ever got a girl pregnant he wanted to be with her because he want to raise his child with both of the parents." So what he gone do about his fiance? "He's gonna break things off with her and try to work things out with me and him." Well how do you feel about that? "I want to be with him I care about him and he is my child's father." Well let me ask you a question then? "What's that?" Do you think he would want to be with you if you wasn't pregnant? "I don't know. He say he care about me." Do you believe him? "I think he do." Well if you happy I'm happy for you guys then do your thing. "So how was your day at work with the doctor?" It was funny as hell. "What happened?" He met my other half. "Tekela?" Yes he did and he didn't even know I had a twin until today. "I bet that fucked his head up." It did. Well I just wanted to stop by to make sure you was OK I got some stuff I got to take care of. Don't forget the party Saturday at Kiera house. "I got to find me something to wear." Me too I'll talk to you later.

When I made it home Antonio mother was outside with the kids. I got out of my truck and started walking toward the steps. "Excuse me can we talk for a minute?" Sure. She walked over to me. "Can we talk woman to woman?" Sure what is it? "It's about my son he is an happily married man with kids and a career. He doesn't need his neighbor to interfere in his marriage." Excuse me! "I see how you and my son look at each other." Me and your son are just friends. "Let me tell you something sweet heart I know your type." What do you mean you know my type? "Girls like you will fuck up an happy home if they want the man." Well mother dear let me tell you something if the happy home is happy even a woman like me can't fuck that up. "I love my son and my daughter in law and I will not stand by and let a woman like you fuck up they home." You know what Mrs. Jackson I'm not the disrespectful type and I'm gone try to keep it respectful because me and your son are friends. But don't come to me like that disrespect me. And if you want to talk more about this anymore you take this up with your son. "Like I said keep your hands off my son." And who are you? "I'm his mother." And you know what mom even you can't stop him from what the fuck he want to do. "I tell you one thing if you fuck up my sons marriage you gone have to deal with me. I will not have my daughter in law coming here insecure about her marriage because she live next door to a slut." I'm gone act like I didn't hear that but see I could be a bitch right now and curse your ass out but I'm not gone do that. If you daughter in law come here and I make her feel insecure about her marriage she shoulda kept her man in Dallas. Because we ATL women we don't give a fuck if we want something we going to get it. "So what are you trying to tell me you gone fuck my son?" Wouldn't you like to know.

I walked in my house and closed my door. She got some fucking nerves approaching me about her son. Only if she knew I was already fucking him. Let me cool off because I'm not gone let his mother upset my nerves. I went upstairs and took a bath after I finished I laid across the bed and went to sleep. My phone rung I turned over and looked at it.

Me:	Hello.
Antonio:	Hey there. Was you asleep?
Me:	Yeah I was.
Antonio:	Do you want me to let you go?
Me:	No I might as well get up. What time is it?
Antonio:	About six thirty.
Me:	How long you been off work?
Antonio:	A lil over an hour.
Me:	Where your mom at?
Antonio:	In the kitchen cooking.
Me:	Did she tell you about our talk we had?
Antonio:	No. What happened?
Me:	Since she didn't tell you I won't say anything.
Antonio:	Don't do that tell me what she say to you.

Me:	You are a happy married man and she don't want me to have anything to do with you.
Antonio:	My mom told you that?
Me:	She sure did.
Antonio:	I'm sorry baby.
Me:	You don't have to apologize. Maybe your mom is right maybe I should leave you alone and let you stay focus on your wife and kids.
Antonio:	My mom already know what's going on with me and my wife. We not as happy as she say we are.
Me:	Every marriage has their problems. She also told me if she find out I'm fucking you I'm gone have to deal with her.
Antonio:	She just looking out for me.
Me:	I understand that cause that's your mom but I'm the wrong one for her to approach, but it's all good I'm not gone trip on it.
Antonio:	I can't believe you got a twin sister and you didn't tell me about it.
Me:	I was gone tell you about it.
Antonio:	Is it anything else you haven't told me?
Me:	No.
Antonio:	Where is your parents?
Me:	Our parents are deceased.
Antonio:	I'm sorry to hear that. So tell me about Mr. McGee.
Me:	What about him?
Antonio:	He like you.
Me:	What makes you think that?
Antonio:	I can tell the way he was watching at you today. He couldn't take his eyes off you. And to be honest with you that shit was pissing me the fuck off.

I started laughing.

Me:	Why did it piss you off?
Antonio:	You belong to me.

Me:	I do.
Antonio:	Yes you do. Mr. McGee will not get his hands on you. Have y'all ever slept together?
Me:	No we have not.
Antonio:	So how do you feel about him?
Me:	I think he is an wonderful doctor. He is sexy and he is funny.
Antonio:	So why come you haven't got with him?
Me:	At the time he was trying to get with me I was already talking to someone.
Antonio:	So what's stopping you from talking to him now.
Me:	I'm fucking you unless you want me to fuck Mr. McGee.
Antonio:	Hell nawl I don't want you to give him my goodies! When is your birthday?
Me:	Saturday.
Antonio:	Your birthday this Saturday and you didn't tell me!
Me:	I forgot.
Antonio:	How you gone forget about something that important I may want to do something special for you.
Me:	I'm sorry.
Antonio:	So what are you going to do for your birthday?
Me:	Me and my sister are having a party at our best friend house.
Antonio:	I'm not invited?
Me:	I didn't think you wanted to come.
Antonio:	What makes you think that?
Me:	You have a wife and the people from the hospital will be there.
Antonio:	And!
Me:	I just didn't think you would want to come.
Antonio:	Well think again I do want to come celebrate your birthday with you. So am I invited?
Me:	Yes you can come. What is you gone tell your mom?

Antonio:	I'm not gone tell her nothing it ain't her business where I'm going I'm a grown ass man. So tell me what do you want for your birthday?
Me:	Surprise me.
Antonio:	Well I'm gone to do just that then. Do you like surprises?
Me:	Yes I do.
Antonio:	Well I'm gone go in here and eat some dinner and see do the kids have some homework and I'm gone talk to you later.
Me:	OK.

I got up and fixed me some dinner called my sister and told her what happened with me and Antonio mom. "Damn that was messed up do she know for a fact y'all fucking?" No she don't. She just assume we fucking. "So what are you going to do?" I'm not gone do shit but keep doing me. "Girl your ass is crazy." Why do I have to be crazy? "Just be careful OK his mother is involved now."

Me and Tekela been talking for about thirty five minutes my other line beep I clicked over it was Kiera. "What are you doing?" Talking to my sister. "Well call me I want to talk to y'all." I told my sister to hold on that was Kiera she want to join the conversation. I linked her in. Kiera let me tell you what happen to me today. Me and Antonio mother had some words. "Are you serious?" Yes! "About what?" She assume me and Antonio fucking. "I don't mean no harm Shekela but mama she can stay out of this cause Antonio is a grown ass man." I agree with you. My sister said "At the end of the day that is still her son and she loves him." That may be true but his mama can't fuck him like Shekela. "You got that right." We all started laughing. I tell you one thing the best thing his mom can do is stay out of this. Because mama can't stop me from doing what I'm already doing. As we was talking I heard a knock on the kitchen door. I got up looked out the blind. Damn y'all speaking of the devil. "Who is it?" Antonio. Let me call y'all back.

I opened the door. "Are you surprise to see me?" As a matter of fact I am. "Why?" It's a work night your mom there. How did you manage to get out the house? "I told her I was going to the hospital to take care some business. I need to see you because I been wanting to do this to you all day long." What's that? "Kiss you." We started kissing he put his hands on my ass start rubbing those cheeks. He picked me up and sat me on top of the kitchen counter and spread my legs wide open. Took off my shirt and went inside the refrigerator and got some whip cream and spread it all over my nipples my thighs my pussy he placed his luscious lips on my nipples, and begin to pull them. I started moaning. He placed three of his fingers inside of my tight pussy pushing his head in and out of it. He placed his tongue in my mouth we started rotating our tongues together. Put his fingers in my mouth and let me taste my own cream. Damn this shit taste sweet. He got on his knees put my legs over his shoulder he started french kissing them fat ass pussy lips. I grabbed the back of his head and pushed it deeper inside of my pussy. I can feel the cum dripping between my ass cheeks. I laid back on the kitchen counter put my legs over my head he stuck his tongue in the crack of my ass and started fucking me. I started biting my nipples calling his name. "Tell me who pussy is this?" This is your pussy Antonio. "Tell me you not gone fuck nobody else." I promise I'm not Antonio. As he was fucking me in the ass with his tongue he had his fingers in my pussy pushing in and out. I was skeeting cum everywhere. "Damn baby look at the way that pussy shoot cum I got to put my dick in there for a few minutes without a condom on." He picked me up and laid me across the floor, took off his clothes got on top of me and worked that dick head inside that wet ass pussy. "Got damn you got all that cum on my dick head. That's it baby push that dick in that pussy come on I know you want to damn Shekela girl don't you make me cum in this pussy come on baby fuck me." Come on Antonio fuck me. He started bouncing up and down in this pussy calling my name begging me not to stop fucking him. I wrapped my legs around his back put my arms around his neck and I started fucking the shit out of him. "Oh baby that's it fuck me Shekela come on fuck me baby. Girl you finna make me nut in this pussy come on baby let it go fuck me. Oh Shekela I'm finna cum Shekela. Oh shit girl." He exploded all in that tight wet pussy. I can feel his whole body just trembling. "Damn woman ain't nobody ever made me cum that hard." Good pussy I make you cum that hard. He pulled his dick out my pussy and started to rub the cum all over my face. He stuck his dick in my mouth and watch me lick the cum off of it. "Damn girl what you trying to do drive a man crazy?" I just want to make you feel good that's all. "I need to get clean up before I go back to the house." We got up and went upstairs took a shower together. We started washing each other body down with bubbles. He quickly grabbed me and pushed my head down pushed his dick in my tight ass pussy. The fuck was on. Water was splashing everywhere from that fuck he was giving me. We both was moaning our asses off. Right before he got ready to get that nut he quickly pulled his dick out and nutted on my ass. "Damn baby look at all this cum on your ass coming out my dick."

We ended up taking another shower together after we finished he got dressed he check his phone the wife had called him four times. I walked him to the door. "You make it hard for a man to leave you." I smiled. We kissed each other. "I'm gone call you when I get settled in OK." OK.

When he made it to the house his mother looked at him. "Where have you been?" To the hospital. "You haven't answered your phone your wife been calling." I know I left my phone in the car. Are the kids sleep? "Yes they are." He went into his bedroom and closed the door and called his wife. Hey sweetie. "Where have you been I been calling you for an hour." I been at the hospital is everything OK? "Everything is fine how was your first day?" Long I'm tired. "Antonio." Yes sweetie. "I miss you." I miss you too baby. "Before you go to sleep hug and kiss the kids for me." OK. When he hung up he walked to the window. Damn I thought she would have the blinds open so I can look at her. She got my mind so fucked up right now. Let me pull myself together before this woman have me losing my mind. If you ain't never have someone to fuck you like she do me you would definitely get unfocused. A woman like her will turn a man world upside down. I can't believe I been here four days and my whole world is upside down. I'm doing something that I didn't think I would end up doing and that's cheating on my wife. Even though we have our problems the sex ain't all that but how could I let a woman I just met four days ago rock my fucking world. I love my wife she is the mother of my kids what I'm doing I know it's wrong I don't want to hurt her, but if I keep fucking this woman next door to me my marriage gone come to an end. Can I live with that?

Over the next several days we had not had a chance to get our freak on the hospital definitely keeps him busy. Me, my sister, Kiera, and Alexandria been getting everything ready for the party Saturday. Passing out the invitations, getting the food and liquor together, the decorations as well.

When we see each other at the hospital we smiled at one another. We text each other back and forth when we get a chance. It's Friday payday. Everybody is excited about that. I was walking down the hall way doctor McGee came up behind me "Thank you for the invitation for the party." You welcome. "So Shekela tell a doctor what can I do for you to make your birthday even more special." I laughed at him. Antonio walked up. "Hey Antonio I just asked Shekela what could I do to make her birthday more special for her." Antonio just looked at him. Dr. McGee the only thing you can do for my birthday is to bring two gifts one for me and one for my sister. "That's not a problem because I love buying gifts for beautiful women." Antonio looked at me. "Shekela can I talk to you for a minute?" Sure. Well I will see you at the party tomorrow night Dr. McGee. "You sure will with your sexy self." I could tell Antonio was pissed off. "Why are you flirting with him in front of my face?" I am not doing that. "That man is gone make me go off on him." You can't do that. "Why come I can't?" We are in the hospital you are married no one here knows we fucking. "Look I'm sorry I just don't like the way he looks at you." Well how do you think I feel every time I look up around a nurse talking about you. How fine and sexy you are. "I don't care anything about that the only person I'm concerned about is you. So who invited him to the party? You?" No my sister did. "What are you finna do now? It's three o'clock." I'm finna get out of here I got some stuff I got to do for the party tomorrow. "You have no idea how bad I want to kiss you right now but I know I can't." No you can't but I will talk to you later.

As I was getting into my truck my cell phone rung it was my sister. "Where are you?" Just leaving the hospital. And you? "On my way to the beauty shop." Well I'll see you there in about twenty minutes.

When I walked through the door Kiera and Alexandria was also there. I guess everybody is getting beautiful for tomorrow night. Kiera asked all of us "Have you girls found something to wear tomorrow?" We all replied no we have not. "Well I guess when we leave the beauty shop we all got to head to the mall." Well I can't speak for you ladies but I want something so hot and sexy and erotic that when Antonio walked through the door all eyes gone be on me. "I thought Antonio wasn't coming?" He asked me when was my birthday I wasn't gone lie to him. I told him Saturday and we was having a party. Alexandria said "Well the doctor gone be in the house damn you ain't gone be able to do shit." The only thing I want to do is the doctor. We all started laughing. Tekela if Antonio ask you did you invite Dr. McGee tell him yes. "Why?" Because I told him you invited him. "Why you gone put me in the middle of this?" Because he know Dr. McGee likes me. Kiera said "Damn you doing Dr. McGee too?" Hell no. He is trying to get the goodies and Antonio can't stand that. Kiera stated "So is Dr. McGee off limits?" No. "What do you mean no?" I'm gone use him to make Antonio jealous. "Now wait a minute Shekela you are playing a dangerous game because those guys work together." I don't care anything about that I'm not trying to fuck Dr. McGee I just want to use him to make Antonio jealous. "We all hear what you saying but that shit can also backfire on your ass." Well I hope not cause everybody in the hospital gone know me and Antonio fucking then. Kiera said "You're a bad ass woman." Alexandria replies "I swear y'all I want to be just like Shekela one day." I tell you ladies one thing you can say I'm wrong all day long but when it comes down to a man if you ain't on top of your game they ass will play you to the tee and swear up and down you are the only one they fucking. I'm not just speaking about me this is for all the ladies if you don't get them they will damn sho will get you and you can be good as hell to them give them all the pussy and head they want, cook, clean, pay the bills, and have a career and that's still not enough for some of them. But I'm not saying all guys are dogs because they not. The only thing I'm saying they got the good ones and the bad ones. I just rather be the one whose doing the playing then get played. Kiera said "I agree I don't want to get played either but Shekela you are playing a dangerous game with the doctor." Well I tell you one thing Kiera Dr. McGee just trying to get some pussy he fuck around with me and he will get fucked big time. Because I will use his ass and throw his ass in the fire. And he still won't get the pussy.

After we finished getting our hair, nails, and toes done we headed to the mall trying on several outfits trying to see which on we gone end up with. Me I needed something to blow Antonio's mind away. I found the perfect dress and matching shoes. I'ma look so good they gone call 911 to put out the fire.

As we were walking out the mall, I bumped right into Antonio. "Well hey ladies." We all spoke. "I guess you getting your shopping on?" I am. "What are you doing here?" Looking for something special. "Well did you find it?" I did. "Well you ladies have a good afternoon." He walked off. Everybody said "Damn Shekela I see why you doing what you doing?" Kiera said "Girl that man fine as hell." I know. Alexandria said "Shekela do he fuck as good as he look?" He so good at what he does make you call your own damn name out. They all started laughing. My sister said "You so fucking scandalous girl its ridiculous." You want to be just like me don't you? "No I don't because you gone make a man do something real bad to you." Not if I don't fuck they ass up first. Well I'm gone talk to y'all later I'm gone go home. Kiera said "Are you going home to fuck Antonio." Maybe maybe not. I laughed as I walked away.

"I really do feel sorry for my sister." Alexandria said "Why?" She gone run up on the wrong one or the wrong wife or somebody gone seriously hurt her. I love my sister and I don't want to see anything to happen to her. But she really do need to slow her roll. "Well you know what you can't be mad at her because she gone do her no matter what we say she still gone do what she want to do." You right she is. I just hope and pray it don't cost my sister her life.

Chapter 4

When I made it home I went into the living room turn on the t.v and watched the news and ate my dinner. When I finished I took me a hot shower and climbed in the bed wondering what Antonio is doing right now.

Antonio. "Yes mom." Don't you think you need to get on the phone and call your wife and tell her to get her soon as she can. "What are you talking about?" I don't like or trust your neighbor. "Are we on this again?" Yes we are because I see the way you and her look at each other y'all are working together everyday. And every time that heffa get out her truck she looking over here at your house. Is it something going on that you not telling your mother. "You reading to much into this mom." No I'm not because I know she told you we had a talk. "She haven't told me anything when did y'all have a talk." Don't worry about all that get on the phone and tell your wife to get home. "I don't get you this is my neighbor she haven't did anything to you why you got some issues with her." Because I know she is a home wrecker I can feel it. It's just something about her I just can't put my finger on it right now I don't trust her. "Well she hasn't did anything to me I think she is nice person." You would think that. "And what do you mean about that." I see the way y'all look at each other a mother knows what she is talking about, Antonio and if your wife had any sense she would get her ass here soon as possible. "Mom you know I have the most up respect for you but please do not call my wife and tell her this mess." This ain't no mess look your mother in the face and tell me you're not attracted to that woman. "She's a very attractive doesn't mean I want to sleep with her. I'll be back." Where you going? "To the hospital I left my cellphone in my office." He gets into his car and drives off. He goes into his pocket and grab his phone. My cellphone rung. Hello. "Are you busy?" No I'm not. "Can you believe me and my mother got into it about you?" What about me? "She think we're sleeping together." What makes her think that? "I have no ideal." What did she say? "She think I should get on the phone and call my wife and tell her to get here." Are you serious? "Yes I am." Well didn't you tell her we wasn't sleeping together. "Yes I told her that my mom have a mind of her own. But for now on when we hook up we gone have to go to a hotel room cause she can be nosy as hell." Well where you at now? "Riding around." Do you think she gone say anything to your wife? "I don't think so I don't want to talk about this anymore I want to talk about you. What are you doing?" Laying in bed. "What do you have on?" Nothing. "Damn you made my dick jump." That ain't all I can do to your dick. "Trust and believe me baby girl I know you a freak." So what are you finna do now? "I'm gone go back to the house unless you want me to stop by." As bad as I wanna say yes I'm gone have to say no. "Why no?" I want to save it for tomorrow night. "Are you excited about your birthday tomorrow." Yes I am. "I still can't believe you got a twin sister." Is it true what they say about a man. "It all depends on what it is." Is it every man fantasy to fuck two twins or two women at the same time. He started laughing. "I can't speak for everybody but it's not my fantasy because if I got one woman giving me everything in the bedroom I don't need nothing else. Is that what you wanna do?" What's that? "Have a man fuck you and your sister." I don't think you or no other man can handle me and my sister together especially me. "Well you may be telling the truth about that I'm a man and I barely can handle you my damn self." He started laughing. "Is your sister a freak too?" I don't think so she may get down with some things but she ain't freaky as me. "I don't think they come no freakier than your ass." Well you better get back to the house before your mom be worried about you trying to figure out who pussy you trying to get into. "My mom gone be OK. I keep trying to tell you I'm a grown ass man." I know what you keep telling me but that's your mom. "You're right she is but my mama can't do what you do to me." You're right about that. "I show wouldn't mind coming through that back door and rubbing my nose between that fat pussy." Goodbye Antonio. "All you gone hang up on me?" No I said goodbye. "You don't want me to." It's not that I just want to save it for tomorrow. "I feel you on that." Did you get your invitation off your desk? "I got it every time I talk to you or see you my dick get hard. I don't want you to think I want to fuck every time I see you but you just do something to me." Well the feelings are mutual because every time I see you or talk to you my pussy get wet. "Damn your pussy wet now?" She sure is. "You got my dick touching the stirring wheel." Your ass is crazy. "I'm telling you the truth though." His phone beep. "Baby girl let me call you back." Why. "This the wife." OK.

"What are you doing?" Just leaving the hospital I left my cell phone in the office and I had to go back to get it. What about you? "Nothing thinking about my husband wondering what are you doing? Don't you want to come to Dallas tomorrow and spend some time with me?" I can't. "Why not?" I'm on call tomorrow at the hospital. "You can't get nobody to cover for you." Baby I just started this job. "I thought maybe you would want to come here and make love to your wife." I do but I can't. "Well I'll be there in another week and I guess I can get all the sex I want then." Well are you finish taking care of your business there. "Just about. How the kids doing in school?" They doing good. "How is your mom?" Mom is being mom. "What do you mean about that?" Nothing. Have you talked to mom? "A couple days ago." Well I'm just pulling in the drive way let me get in the house and take a shower and get ready for bed and I'm gone talk to you later. "Antonio I love you." I love you too. He hung up damn I wonder have my mom talked to her. She want me to come and see her I can't do that. Ain't no way in the hell I'm gone miss out on what's gone happen tomorrow night.

I was coming out my front door to take the trash out to the garbage, Antonio was getting out his car his mother was standing in the front door. We look at each other smiled and we spoke. His mom just look at me and rolled her eyes. I started laughing at her I knew that would piss her off. Goodnight Antonio. "Goodnight Shekela." I know that wrecked her fucking nerves.

Mom what are you doing? "Why are you speaking to her?" Just gone in the house and quit trying to start problems. "Me starting problems? You really don't see whats going on in front of you do you?" Now what are you talking about? "That hoe next door gone be the reason your marriage gone fall apart don't say your mama didn't tell you so." Why you calling her a hoe? "Because that's what she is I can see it." If you stop judging her you would come to see she is a nice person. "Aw you defending the hoe now." Will you please keep your voice down my kids are in the house. I'm not finna argue with you about this goodnight mother.

I got up open my blinds turn off the light and lit some candles and put on some soft music. Antonio went into his room and lock the door. He notice I had my blinds open. He walked over to the window. I was walking around my bedroom ass naked he hurried up and called me. "You have no idea how bad I needed this." Are you OK? "I'll tell you about it later but just keep doing what you doing I'm just gone sit back and watch." I grabbed a chair, sat down in front of the window, spread my legs wide open and let him watch me play with my fat pussy. He started taking off his clothes. He grabbed a chair and I watched him play with his big dick. We sat there and masturbated in front of each other for about an hour. When we finished he called me. "I can get used to this every night watching you play with your pussy." Do you want to see me suck the cum off my fingers? "Ooohhh yes indeed." One by one I put finger in my mouth and lick the cum off them. You want to see me do something else? "Yes." I got up and bend over made my ass cheeks clap up and down. "Got damn I haven't never seen no shit like that the next time we together that is the way I want you to make your ass cheeks juggle on my dick." I will do whatever you want me to do as long as you stick your dick in my tight ass and fuck me. "Damn you get down like that?" Yes, I want you to nut all in my ass hole. "If you keep talking to me like that I'm coming to your back door." Well we better stop because I'm holding the goodies till tomorrow night. "Girl you got my dick so hard it don't make no sense." Well you better go take a cold shower and cool off. "I'm gone have to I can't go to sleep like this." Well you go handle your business I'm gone go to bed because I have a long day tomorrow. "Well I'm gone call you in the morning then OK." OK baby. "Goodnight sexy." Goodnight. After we hung up I got back in bed laughing to myself I got him just how I want him and I went to sleep.

It was Saturday morning about eight o'clock. My house phone and cellphone start ringing its ass off. Everybody was calling to wish me a happy birthday. About eight thirty the door bell rung. I went downstairs and opened it. Some has sent a dozen of red roses and about twenty balloons with happy birthday on it. I open the card it was from Antonio. I text his phone and told him thank you. My phone rung it was my sister. "Well happy birthday Shekela." Well happy birthday to you too Tekela. "So what did the doctor get you?" He sent me a dozen of roses and twenty balloons with happy birthday on it. "Well that was sweet." He is a sweet person. Well we better get up we got a lot of stuff to get done before eight o'clock. Well I will meet you at Kiera house in bout an hour. "OK."

After I got dressed and grabbed some breakfast I head to Kiera house. We all got together and did the decorations. Alexandria said "Well Kiera tell us did you and the doctor fuck last night." No we didn't we had open window sex last night. Kiera said "What the hell is that." He sat in front of his window and I sat in front of mines and we watch each other masturbate for bout an hour. They all started laughing. Kiera said "Maybe I should try that shit. Girl Tekela your sister know some freaky ass shit to do that's why all them men going crazy." That's why everybody want to be like Shekela now I'm going to the liquor store Alexandria you come on roll with me. While we doing this y'all go to the store and get the rest of the stuff we need for the party we got a lot of shit to do.

So Alexandria tell me more about your situation. "Awl yeah girl he broke things off with her and he move in with me last night." Does he seem happy about the baby? "He say he is." Are you guys going to get married? "He want to say he want to do the right thing take care of his family." Well that's a good brother then, well I hope everything works out for y'all. "He also coming to the party with me tonight." OK. When we got to the liquor store we picked up everything we needed and headed back to the house. When we got back they pick up the cake and got all the food together. We had a lot of cooking to do so we put on some music and made some drinks. Over the next five hours all we did was cook laugh and played around and getting everything together for tonight. Chris came by and brought the barbecue ribs, the chicken, and the fish. Come in for a minute and have a drink with us. We had several people stopping by and dropping off food. It was about six o'clock it was time for us to go home and get ready.

When I made it there I can see Antonio wasn't there yet. He must be still at work. I got in took a hot bath and start getting ready. I did my make up I put my red thong on my stilettos and this bad ass dress I bought. The dress was red short if I bend over they ain't gone see nothing but pussy. Had all the back out showing my titties it was off the hook I was looking good, smelling good, and damn sho taste good. I should know because I love tasting my cream. When I was walking out the door heading to my truck

I seen Antonio mother standing in the door way looking at me. From the look on her face I know she wanted to say something to me but she didn't smart woman.

When I got back to Kiera house and walked through the door everybody said "Damn Shekela are you trying to start a fire?" You damn Skippy. Alexandria showed up with her boyfriend Keshun. We congratulate them. We got the party started people started showing up. They was coming in wishing us a happy birthday everybody was bringing gifts. Dr. McGee just showed up hugging us wishing us a happy birthday. "Tekela you look very nice." Thank you. "Shekela girl you look so good in that dress make a brother heart skip a beat." I laughed at him. "Shekela come on and slow dance with me so I can fantasize about being with you." Dr. McGee don't be trying to rub my booty. "I want to do something else to them ass cheeks." As we was slow dancing Antonio walked through the door looking around he spotted my sister walked up to her "Happy birthday." Thank you. And gave her gift. "Where your sister?" She may be in the kitchen but I'm not sure. He started walking around talking to people but in reality he was looking for me he found me on the floor slow dancing. When the song was over he walked up to me "Well happy birthday Shekela." Thank you. "Well can I have the next dance?" Sure. We started slow dancing. "You look delicious." You think so. "I hope Dr. McGee didn't have his hands all over you." Don't worry about it he didn't. "Did you like your roses and your balloons?" I did thank you so much. "That's just one of your surprises you get your other one later. You smell good!" And I taste good too. "I know you do." Kiera walked up to my sister "I guess Antonio found her." How do you know? They slow dancing together.

Are you hungry? "Yes but not for food." Come on let me get you something to eat and drink. Here go your plate I will be back. "Where you going?" I got to go mingle remember its my birthday. "How long you gone be gone?" Not long.

We had a nice crowd everybody was enjoying their self. My homeboy Anthony showed up he brought gifts. He ask me to dance with him. I did. Antonio couldn't take his eyes off me. I could see he was pissed off because Anthony was all on my ass. My sister, Alexandria, and Kiera was watching me. Kiera said "Humph your sister love playing them dangerous games don't she? Antonio can't take his eyes off her ass while she out there dancing." Alexandria reply "That's what she want and I don't blame her." Kiera said "I'm gone go over here and stand next to Antonio and talk to him." Alexandria "I'm gone go with you come on. What about you Tekela?" I'll pass I don't to have anything to do with this.

Well hey Antonio are you enjoying the party? "Yes I am." We see you can't take your eyes off Shekela. "Who is that guy she dancing with?" Aw that's her best friend Anthony they grew up together. "Y'all know about us don't you?" She told us a lil something. "I think y'all know everything." Alexandria started laughing. Kiera said "Well Antonio don't be embarrassed about it because she a beautiful woman and guys just fall in love with her. "She is breathtaking and you're right I can't keep my eyes off of her." After me and Anthony got through dancing Dr. McGee grabbed me by the hand and pulled me to the floor and we started dancing. Antonio looked at Kiera "I don't like him." Why you don't like him? "He trying to push his self all up on my girl, and that's what he trying to do me and him gone have a problem." Kiera just looked at him you know they just friends. "That's what she told me but I think he want more than just friends with her and if that's what he want it ain't gone happen not as long as I'm in the picture."

About an hour later it was time for us to cut the birthday cake. Everybody gathered around and started singing happy birthday to me and my sister. We blew out the candles made a wish and cut the cake. Chris said "Can I have everyone attention I want to make a toast to Shekela and Tekela I want to wish you guys a happy birthday and I hope you got everything you wished for. I love you with all my heart y'all just like my sisters. So everybody raised their glass. On the count of three everybody say happy birthday. One, two, three. Happy birthday Shekela and Tekela from all of us."

It's about eleven thirty Antonio found me and ask me to come outside with him. "I know this your birthday party but I was wondering can I steal you away for the rest of the night?" What do you have in mind? "You gotta come with me." Well let me tell my sister them good night and I will be right back.

I didn't see my sister but I found Kiera. I'm finna get ready to go and I will see y'all tomorrow. "Where you going?" With Antonio. "Aw hell I know what y'all going to do." Put some cake and food up and I will come by and get it tomorrow. "Well you have a good birthday." Trust me I plan on it.

Chapter 5

I got in the car he drove off. You not gone tell me where we going. "I don't want to spoil your surprise you just got to wait and see." We pulled up in front of a hotel. We looked at each other. "You ready for your surprise?" Yes! We got out the car he grabbed me by the hand and we went to our room. "I need you to stay right here for a minute." Why? "I got something to do before you come in." OK. He went inside and close the door. What is he doing inside I been standing out here for five minutes. He finally open the door. "Close your eyes." He grabbed my hand and pulled me into the room and close the door behind us. "Now open your eyes beautiful." Wow! You went through all this trouble for me? "It was no trouble I wanted to do something special for you." This is so romantic you got candles lit everywhere, rose petals all over the bed, champagne on ice. Thank you. "You are so welcome beautiful. I got one more surprise for you. Happy birthday baby." When I open the box it was a pair of diamond earrings. Aw Antonio these are beautiful. "Not as half as beautiful as you are." You brought me diamonds. "Well diamonds are a girls best friend." I hugged and kiss him. You are so romantic. "You did this to me." What? "Knock the romance out of me and the freak as well. There is nothing I wouldn't do for you Shekela I know you might not want to hear this right now but I got to tell you I think I'm falling in love with you." I looked at him. Are you sure about that? "Yes I am." Well I got a confession myself Antonio I'm falling for you as well. "I promise you Shekela I'm not gone hurt you." Please don't. We started kissing. Are you gone be able to stay out all night? "I'm not going nowhere baby this is your special day and I want to spend it with you." What about your mom? "Let me worry about that we not gone talk about my mom. All I want to do is make love to you. Kiss you from head to toe lick you from front to back." Well you better get started then. He grabbed me by my face kiss me on my forehead, my nose, my cheeks. "You smell so good." Nibbling on my ear, lick me all around my neck I started moaning. He got down on his knees kissing my legs, licking my thighs, put his head under my dress, kissing me all between my pussy lips. I put my right leg over his shoulder. Aw Antonio oh don't stop. He was eating the pussy so good my legs went to shaking. I damn near fell on the floor. He grabbed me pick me up laid me on the bed he took off my shoes and my dress. I pulled his shirt off and unbuckled his pants. He slowly started taking off my shoes sucking on my toes kiss me in the bottom of my feet. I had my eyes closed I felt something cold on my stomach I open up my eyes and look down. He had peaches and cream all on my stomach. He started licking and eating it.

The party started winding down everybody was leaving. My sister asked Kiera "Where is Shekela?" I forgot to tell you she left with Antonio. "She left her own party?" Hell yeah she left and I don't blame her she gone to get her freak on. Chris walked up "Where is Shekela at I been looking for her." Aw she left. "She left her own party?" She had to take care of something. "Tekela what's wrong with you?" Nothing. "Well is she coming back?" I don't think so. "Wait something don't seem right Shekela leaving her birthday party. It must be a dick involved." They laughed. "So Kiera tell me we all know you can't hold water." What do you mean I can't hold water? "Who did she leave here with?" Shekela is a grown ass woman. "I know she grown but you still ain't told me who she left the party with." I don't know. "I find that hard to believe."

After he finished licking my stomach up and down he started sucking the bottom of my lip placed his tongue inside of my mouth. I flipped his ass over jumped on top of him beginning to bit his nipples lick him in his chest, caressed his stomach with my tongue. I took the whip cream and spread it on the inside of my hand and took it and rubbed his dick and balls with it. I open up his legs place my tongue between the crack of his ass blew all in it. I could hear him call my name as I was licking the whip cream off his balls. I placed my tongue on the tip head of his dick and started licking sucking on the head of it like it was a lollipop. I could feel his whole body trembling as my mouth went deeper down on his dick. He grabbed my head and begin to push it up and down on his dick. I could feel the warm cum coming out that's when I start deep throating that dick. I could feel it hitting the back of my throat as I was swallowing the cum down he got so loud begging me "Don't leave him don't give this pussy to nobody else please baby." I was sucking the dick so good he called out his own damn name. The people in the next room begin to knock on the wall asking us to come the noise down because we was screaming and hollering so loud. He was pushing my head up and down on his dick so good he thought he was getting the pussy. He exploded all in my mouth. He looked at me "Get up baby I want to get this shit from the back." I got up bend over and grabbed my ankles he stood behind me. "Boy you sho was blessed with ass on you." He kissed my ass cheek took his hand start clapping them got on his knees took his hand and spread my ass cheeks wide open and placed his tongue in that ass hole and fucked it like he was fucking the mouth. "Shekela!" Yeah baby? "I want to know can I stick my dick in your ass hole." I looked back at him you don't have to ask me anything this body belong to you. You do what you want to do to it. He got up begin to push one of his fingers in my ass hole to open it up. He slowly rubbed his dick head between my ass. "I never done this before I don't want to hurt you." It's OK just take your time don't be in a rush. He started working it in real slow. "Damn girl I can't believe I'm doing this shit you got a fat as ass." I can feel the pressure from his dick entering my ass hole. It took him about ten minutes to get it in but once he got in all hell broke loose. He started pushing it in and out. I was slapping my ass cheeks on that dick when he was fucking me. His cell phone rung. You want to stop and get that? "Ain't no way in the hell I'm finna stop this shit keep bouncing that ass on my dick." It was the wife wondering where he was. She called the house phone, his mother got it. "Hey mom is Antonio at home?" No baby he is not here. Did you call his cellphone? "I did he didn't pick up." Did you call the hospital and have him paged? "I did that too they say he was gone. I can't believe he not at home and it's one thirty in the morning." His mom got up and looked out the window. Thinking to her self this heifer ain't at home either. Mariah let me tell you something baby. "What's that mom?" You need to get here. "What is you talking about?" Y'all next door neighbor. "Aw we have a neighbor?" Antonio didn't tell you about her. "No he didn't what about her?" She been flirting with your husband and giving him that come fuck me look. "Are you serious?" Yes I am. Me and that heifer had a few words. "About what?" It's not important you just need to get here if you want to save your marriage. "Ma I'm not insecure you know

Antonio don't cheat." I know he don't cheat and you know he don't cheat but when you live next door to a hoe you can't say what a man won't do baby. I'm not trying to start anything with you and my son. It's one thirty in the morning he not here I just looked out the window her truck is not here either. "It might just be a coincidence they both out." OK coincidence every time she see Antonio she smiling winking her eye at him dressing half ass naked. "What do she look like?" Honestly? "Yes mom honestly." She is a very beautiful woman and I know her type she look like she a home wrecker and they work everyday too. "What you mean they work together?" She a nurse at the same hospital Antonio work at. If that ain't enough to get your butt her where your husband is nothing is girl. "Don't even tell him I called the house don't even let him know we had this discussion." Are you coming? "Yeah I'm gone surprise him." You better do it quick fast and in a hurry because the slut next door she look like she don't waste no time. "I'll talk to you later mom." OK.

He was fucking me so hard in my ass the cum was dripping down my thigh. He pulled out and started shaking his dick on my ass. I laid across the bed and spread them legs open he reached into his pocket and pulled out a condom. He looked at me "Do you want me to put it on?" I think you should because I'm not on anything. "You just don't know how bad I don't want to." We started kissing he put his dick inside my pussy slowing pushed it in and out put them legs over his shoulder and started fucking me. "Damn baby this pussy feel so good it don't make no sense." That's it Antonio fuck me baby come on fuck me hard that's it baby fuck me. His cellphone rung again. Come on baby that's it fuck me Antonio. He started biting my nipples he was pounding that pussy. "Oh Shekela, that's it. Throw me this pussy, throw this pussy on my dick, girl. That's it. Fuck me." I was fucking his ass so good the harder he fuck me the more I cum. When he finally pulled his dick out he couldn't even see the condom cause I cum so many times on his dick. He looked down "I ain't never seen a woman cum so thick and white like this before damn you got some good ass pussy on you woman." We laid there in bed holding each other. I didn't eat anything at the party but I'm hungry as hell now. "You want me to go out and get you something to eat?" No I'm gone call Kiera and see is she still up and will she bring both of us something to eat all that food we had at the party. I called her. Are you busy? "No but I thought you would be." We started laughing. Everybody gone home? "Yeah it's just me and Alexandria putting everything up." I'm sorry I left you guys to do all the work. "Don't worry about it we knew you had bigger things to take care of." Your ass crazy Kiera. I was wondering would you do me a favor? "What is it?" Would you bring us some food to the hotel? "I guess y'all done fucked up a storm now y'all ass over there hungry." Are you gone do it or what? "Yeah I'm gone bring it where y'all at?" You know that hotel about two blocks from where you live at. "That nice hotel?" Yes we in the room twenty eight hundred. "Damn y'all on the top floor the expensive ass rooms." What you know about these rooms? "I heard about them." Um hmm I bet you did. "We will be there in about twenty minutes." Bring some cake and some liquor if any was left. "I'm gone hook y'all up." Aite girl.

"So she gone bring us something to eat" Antonio said. Yeah that's my girl she gone hook us up. "Well lets go take a shower before she get here because she nosy as hell she might want to come in. We got up took a shower and cleaned the room up a little bit and put our clothes on. You not gone get your phone to see who was calling you. "No." You sure about that? "I got a pretty good idea who it is." The wife? "Yeah." If you want to go home I understand. "I'm not leaving you this is your special day and I want you to enjoy every bit of it."

It was a knock on the door I got up and open it. It was Kiera and Alexandria with a big smile on they face. "Are you gone let us in?" Y'all can come in for a minute. "Hey Antonio." How you ladies doing? "We bought enough food to last y'all until tomorrow and drinks as well." Well I definitely appreciate what y'all did for us. "It's all good you know we got your back." Well I'll see you ladies tomorrow.

After they left we went to the table sat down and started eating. "You have some very special friends." They are they more like my sisters than my friends because we can always depend on one another no matter what the situation is. "It's good to have friends like that." When we finished eating we got in the bed and had a couple of drinks and started talking. I know you don't want to hear that right now but what's gone happen to us when your wife gets here. "We just gone have to take it one day at a time, but I promise you I will find some time for you." I looked at him and kissed him laid my head in his arms and we dosed off and went to sleep.

It was about five thirty the morning his phone rung. He reached over and grabbed it he woke me up and told me he had to go. Is everything OK. "My wife been calling me all night I really don't want to go but I need to." I understand. "Check out time ain't until eleven o'clock won't you just stay to then and I will see you later." OK I will do that. He got dressed and we hugged and kissed. "Did you have a nice birthday?" I did and you made it so special for me. "I wanted it to be special because you are a special woman." Thank you again for the diamond earrings. "You welcome. After he left I got back in bed rolled over and went to sleep.

It was about six thirty he was walking in the door. "Antonio where have you been all night don't you know I been worried." Mom please calm down before you wake the kids up I'm OK. "Now I see you OK and why come you didn't answer your cellphone?" I been out with some friends all night. "And you couldn't answer your phone something could have happened and you would have never known because you didn't answer your phone that's not like you. What was you doing so busy that you couldn't take out the time to answer your phone." Mom please I been working so hard all week and a couple of doctors I work with invited me to a party. "OK Antonio I understand you been working hard all week the only thing I'm saying that you could have pick up the phone and called and let me know you was OK. You know I worry about you." I'm sorry OK I do apologize as well as long as you here helping me with the kids and I decide to stay out all night I will make sure to call you and let you know so you won't be worried. "There is something different about you I don't know what it is but I can tell something is going on with you. Now if you want to sit down and talk to your mom I'm here." It's nothing to talk about I'm fine. "Whatever is going on with you, you better get it together before your wife get here. Do you remember her?" Of course I remember my wife mom I'm going to check on the kids and I'm going to sleep.

My son must forgot I'm a woman too I also been involved with a married man I know all the games she playing with him but I'm not gone stand by and watch this hoe hurt my son and my family. She walked toward the front door and look out the window. What a coincidence she not at home yet either. I'm willing to bet they was together last night and If I find out that slut is fucking my son all hell gone break loose.

Chapter 6

It was about ten o'clock I got up and got dressed and headed home. As I was pulling up his mom and the kids was getting in the car. You kids sit right here don't move. She closed the door.

"Excuse me we need to talk." I looked back. That's where you wrong we don't have a damn thing to talk about. "I may not be able to prove it but I know you was with my son last night." Excuse me! "You heard me." Do you have a husband or a boyfriend because I can tell you don't because you got to much time on your hands. "For your information I have a husband I'm here to help my son out until my daughter in law get here. You better enjoy it while you can because this week I got a surprise for you it's gone fuck up your whole world." Do I look like I'm worried. "You may not be but trust and believe me you will be." Is that a threat? "Take it anyway you want to take it." Mama dearest let me tell you a thing or two you don't know me and I don't think you would like to get to now me because I can be a trifling bitch. "And you know what so can my daughter in law." Well if your daughter in law was taking care her business you wouldn't be over here all up in mine, worried about am I fucking the husband. "If my son is fucking you that's all it is a fuck. And I hope and pray he is not because I raised him to be a man a real man." Even real men fuck up how you know your husband ain't fucking up on you while you all up in my business. "You fucking trash." Well it takes one to know one and I walked away. I went into my house she got in the car and left. This is some crazy as shit. His mother got some fucking nerves approaching me a second time about her son. Now if I was a trifling bitch I would have let her known she late I'm already getting that dick, but I'm not gone do that I got a surprise for her and she ain't gone see it coming. The wife my lease worry because I already know she can't fuck him like me.

59

She want some competition I'm gone give her ass some. I can't wait to see what she look like. I tell you one thing she better be a dime like me if she ain't I feel sorry for her, but the bitch better bring it on. I'm not a loser I'm a winner, and I always come out on top no matter what.

I went upstairs and took a shower and got dressed, as I was walking out the door I reached into my purse and grabbed my cellphone and called Kiera. I'm on my way to your house call my sister and Alexandria and tell them to meet me there I got some shit for y'all ears. "What's going on?" I'll see you in about twenty minutes. My phone rung it was Antonio. "Hey beautiful." Hey sweetie. "Where you at I went outside and I didn't see your truck?" I'm on my way to Kiera house. "Are you OK?" I'm fine but I'm gone call you later OK. "You can't talk to me now?" I got some stuff I got to do but I will talk to you later. "OK."

When I pulled in the drive way they was already there. I walked in the house Kiera said "What the hell is wrong with you?" This heifer again approach me. "Who?" Antonio mother. "Aw shit Alexandria get the drinks we got to sit down and talk about this shit." We got into a big argument outside. "About what?" She think me and Antonio was together last night which we was but that ain't her damn business and the shit was on from there. She gone tell me she got a surprise for me, but what she don't know I got a treat for her ass. My sister said "Did you tell Antonio about this?" No and I'm not gone tell him. "Why not?" I can take care of his mother I don't need him to defend me. "That might be true Shekela but that is his mother." Well you know what then mom better stay in her damn place and stay the fuck out my business, because she fucking with the wrong one. Then she gone tell me if I fuck up her family I'm gone have to answer to her. Kiera said "This sound like soap opera shit enough about the mother tell us about last night." You already know what happen I turned his ass out. "Well we already know that what he get you for your birthday?" Diamond earrings. "Get the hell out of here." Yes he did. "Girl you must be putting that coochie crunch on that man." I got something even better than that. They all said "What's that?" He told me last night he falling in love with me. Everybody just looked at me. My sister said "What you tell him?" I feel the same way. "Do you?" I sure do and I'm not gone let his mama or his wife stop me from getting what I want. "By the way Shekela I put all your birthday presents upstairs in my guest room." I appreciate that Kiera. Alexandria said "I can see the man like you we all can see that. He gave you diamonds took you to an expensive ass hotel last night and I know y'all got y'all damn freak on up in there." We all laughed. "Then he told you how he feel about you. I'm not mad at you do you, but his mom for real for real she do need to stay out of this. That might be her son and she may love her daughter in law and grand kids but Antonio is a grown ass man and not even his mother can stop him from doing what he do." Tekela said "Did you find anything out about his wife?" I did she works at a bank. "When she coming to Atlanta?" Probably the weekend it will be two weeks. "So what you gone do?" Continue to do what I'm doing now and that's fucking her husband. "I just want you to be careful I don't want to see anything happen to you. I know this thing with him started off as a game to you but your feelings got involved. A lot of times when a married man fuck around on his wife the wife always win in the end." But sometimes things can be different too the other woman can also come out on top and that's what I plan on doing.

After we finished talking, drinking, and eating I got all my birthday presents my cake and some food and I headed home. As I was pulling in the drive way I could see Antonio mother is still out. When I got inside I put everything up and called Antonio. What are you doing? "Just waking up what are doing?" I just got back home. "Where you been?" Over to Kiera house to pick up my gifts and something to eat. Where your mom at? "She took the kids to the park for a while." If you hungry I bought enough food for you and me. "You gone put it up so I can come get it later." Why you can't come get it now your mama not there. He started laughing. "Do you want me to come get the food or you just want me to come and fuck you." Just come and get the food. "Meet me at your backdoor." Give me about five minutes. "OK."

After we hung up I rushed downstairs, and I put cake all over on my nipples. There was a knock on the door. When I opened it he had a big ass smile on his face. "Damn dinner I'm coming for dessert." I looked at him I didn't think you was coming over. "Why not?" Because your mom can pop up at any giving time, and that's not gone look good at all. "Right now my mom is the last thing on my mind. My eyes are on them nipples with cake all around them." I didn't invite you over here for sex I do have your dinner. "That might be true. Damn girl you look tasty." I grabbed my t-shirt and put it on. You better get your dinner and go home before you get caught. "You not gone give me any?" Not this time maybe next time. "So you gone send me home with a hard dick?" For sho! "You wrong for that." I know now here go your dinner. Go home and be a good little boy. "I have no choice but to go home and be good." We hugged and kissed.

About twenty minutes later I sent him a text a picture of me playing with my pussy. He text me back "You ain't nothing but a bad freak and I like that." About five minutes later he sent me a text a picture of his dick with cum dripping out of it. We continue to send naked pictures back and forward to one another for about thirty minutes. He text me "My mom just got here I'm gone have to talk to you later."

Over the next couple of days he got so busy at the hospital all we could do was talk on the phone and text each other. It was a Wednesday afternoon I was just getting off work he text me and told me to come into his office before I leave the hospital. As I was getting ready to walk in the door Dr. McGee stop me "Did you like the birthday present I bought for you." Yes I did and thank you so much. "I was looking for you that night." I had something I had to go take care of. "Well I was wondering is it possible for me to take you out Friday night to the movies and dinner?" I'm sorry I would love to go but I can't. "Why not?" I have a boyfriend. "You do?" Yes. Antonio was at the door listening to the conversation. "So that's where you went to." I did. "Did he get you a nice birthday present?" He sure did. "Well I tell you what if things don't work out between you and your boyfriend you let me know." I'll keep that in mind. He walked off. I walked into Antonio office "He gone make me whoop his ass eventually." You wanted to see me. He closed the door and we started kissing. "I miss you." I miss you too. "I been so busy at work I haven't had time for you but tonight I got something very special for you." And what's that? "I want you to meet me at the hotel about seven o'clock I got the same room we had everything is paid for just go to the front desk and get the key. When you get there I got something very sexy laying across the bed for you I want you to have on." I smiled at him. "Well I got some errands I got to run I get off at five o'clock." Well I guess I'll see you at the room. "OK sexy." He slap me on the ass cheek I looked back "I can't wait to get to get my hands on you tonight." Well that makes two of us, because she defiantly need some attention. "Well you let her know daddy gone hook her up tonight." Well I guess I'll see you tonight. "Where you finna go now?" I'm going home to get ready for you. "OK baby girl."

As I was walking in the door my cellphone rung it was Kiera. "What are you doing?" I'm just getting home. "I was calling you to see did you want to come over and we play some cards tonight." I'm gone have to pass up on that because I have a date tonight with Antonio at the hotel. "Oh shit ain't y'all tired of fucking?" No we're not we haven't had any in a couple of days he been busy at the hospital so tonight he said he gone make it very special for me and make up for lost time. "I sho wish I had a man like Antonio." Why is that? "Somebody to give me diamonds take me to an expensive ass hotel. Have you bumped into his mother anymore?" No I haven't but don't speak to soon. "I forgot to tell you something." What's that? "The night of the party when you was dancing with Chris, Antonio was asking me a lot of questions about him. I told him y'all was just friends." I had already told Antonio me and Chris was friends. "Well I guess he didn't like the way Chris was all up on your ass." He will be alright. Let me get up and get ready and I will talk to you later. "Well you have fun." I plan on it.

Walking out the door getting ready to go to the hotel it's about five thirty Antonio hasn't made it home yet. I wanted to get there early. I stop by the store picked up some candles, rose petals and champagne, and made a stop to pick up some Chinese food for dinner.

When he walked through the door his mom and kids was sitting down having dinner. She looked at him "I got dinner waiting on you." I'm sorry I'm not gone be able to stay for dinner. "Why not?" I'm going to hang out with a couple of friends from the hospital. "On a Wednesday night?" Yes. "Are you gone be out all night?" No I'm not just for a few hours mom. He goes upstairs take a shower and get ready.

I got to the hotel room I got the key went inside the room lit candles, put the champagne on ice, and put on this sexy ass lingerie he bought me. I looked at my watch it was about twenty minutes to seven. I can't wait to see my baby so we can make love.

When he came downstairs he gave the kids a hug and kiss and told them he would see them later. His mom looked at him. I'll see you later mom. "OK." He walked outside and got into his car, reached into his pocket and grabbed his cellphone. He sent me a text and said he was on his way. I smiled. As he was getting ready to back out a car pulled up right behind him. He looked back. I know this ain't who I think it is. Hell no. He got out the car. "Hey honey!" His eyes bucked. Hey sweetie what are you doing here. "I came to surprise you." I thought you wasn't coming until Saturday. "I changed my mind I couldn't stay away from my husband to much longer. I miss you." I miss you too. "Where the kids?" In the house you drove by yourself? "No I didn't Brenda is with me she is in the back of the car sleep. Let me wake her up, come and help me get the bags." Thinking to him self I can't believe this shit. Out of all nights she came tonight when I was about to get my freak on with my baby. "Are you happy to see me?" What kind of question is that? "You just don't look happy." Sweetheart I'm just tired, of course I'm happy to see you. "You dressed all up where you finna go?" I was going to hang out with some friends. They all walked in the house. "Hey kids." Mom! His mother had a big ass smile on her face. "Hey mom how you doing?" I'm doing good how you doing? "I'm glad to be with my husband." All you brought Brenda with you. "Yes I did she gone stay with us for a couple of weeks." Antonio just looked at everybody. I looked at my watch again it's seven twenty. Damn he late let me send him a text. As he was standing around talking to everybody his phone went off. His wife looked at him. His mom said "Are you still going to see your friends if so take your wife with you." I would love to meet some of your friends. I think I'm gone cancel. "Why?" You just got in town I want to spend some time with you me and the kids. I got plenty of time to introduce you to my friends.

Damn he has not respond to my text. Let me call him to make sure everything is OK. I called his phone he looked at it he sent me to voice mail. "Dang baby somebody must really want to talk to you they blowing up your phone." Probably the guys calling to see where I'm at. "Well go head and call." I'll call them later I'm gone outside and bring the rest of the bags in the house. "I'll help you."

As he was bringing the bags in "I miss you so much sweetie. I'm just glad I'm here with you now because I defiantly want to make love with my husband tonight." He just looked at her. Only if she knew my mind is somewhere else right now and I know she got to be wondering what the hell is going on why I haven't replied to her text or return her phone call. I got to find a way to either call her or get to her. Some how some way because I don't want my baby girl to be upset with me right now. This is to important to both of us.

About an hour and half has passed by I still have not heard from Antonio so I got up and got dressed. I packed everything up and head to the house. As I was getting close to the house I can see that Antonio car is still in the drive way. I wonder what the hell is going on with him. Who car is that I never seen it before. Maybe something happened.

As I was getting out the truck grabbing everything I seen Antonio come out the door we looked at each other then a woman came behind him she looked at me. She spoke. Antonio looked at her. "Who is that baby?" That's our neighbor Shekela. Hey Shekela. "Hey Antonio." Let me introduce you to my wife Mariah. I had this fucked up look on my face. Damn the wife is here.

Hey how you doing Mariah? "I'm doing pretty good." Moments later his mom walked outside she looked at me with a smile on her face. Mariah have you met your neighbor Shekela? "Yes Antonio just introduced us." Antonio was getting the rest of the bags out the car. I told you she look like a hoe don't see? "Mom stop." Did you see the reaction on her face when he introduced you as his wife? "Yeah I did and from the look of it she was in shock, but we still don't know if they fucking or not mom." Girl please. Brenda came outside "Do y'all need any help getting the bags in?" No Antonio got everything. I just met my new neighbor. "Who is she?" Her name is Shekela. Antonio mom said "And she a hoe at that." "What she look like?" She is a very attracted woman. "Mrs. Jackson how you know she a hoe?" Trust me I can spot a hoe mile away. They all started laughing. Antonio took the bags inside the house. His mom, wife, and sister in law was still outside. As I was changing clothes I peak out the window and I could see them looking at my house. Since they want to look let me give them something to look at. I put on a pair of daisy duke short pants with my ass cheeks out and a see through shirt with no bra on. I grabbed my keys and walked out the door. All eyes was on me. I came out the door switching my ass off. Antonio walked out the door he looked at me. The wife looked at him. I stood in front of my truck went into my purse and grabbed my cellphone and called Kiera. Hey girl what are you doing? "What am I doing? What are you doing? You suppose to be at the hotel with Antonio." I suppose to be but I'm not. "Where are you?" At home. "Is everything OK?" No, but I'm on my way to your house. Get some drinks together cause we gone need one. After I hung up I got in my truck slowly backing out the drive way Antonio was in the truck getting the bags. As I was looking back I looked at him his lips was moving "I'm gone call you later."

"Damn Mrs. Jackson you was right she do look like a hoe." Come on ladies be nice we don't know anything about her. "You speak for yourself I know a lot about her I know her type. You haven't been here while she been winking her eye at your husband coming outside half ass naked. Did you see that shit she had on a while ago?" Mom just calm down. "I'm telling you Mariah you better step your game up because you live next door to a slut. And I can tell you right now y'all gone have some problems." Brenda said "Mariah she is right when you live next door to a hoe will do anything and will fuck anything." Y'all gotta understand one thing though I trust my husband I know he won't cheat on me. "I'm your sister and I always will tell you the truth never say what a man won't do." If you know your husband like I know mines he won't cheat he have no reason to cheat he has a family, career, and a wife who loves him very much. "That may be all good but sometimes even that's not enough for a man." If you know your man like I know mines you ain't got to worry about anything because I know my husband.

I got to Kiera house walked in the door. I need a drink fuck it I need two or three drinks. "What's going on now?" The wife done showed up. "Are you serious?" Yes I am. "When?" Evidently tonight because I was at the hotel waiting on him he didn't show up so I called him text him I didn't get a respond. So I got dressed and went home. I get to the house he introduce me to his wife Mariah. "Girl that's some shit there. What she look like?" The typically ass wife. "Break it down to me give me details." She tall, slim, short hair, she's fuck-able but she ain't got shit on me. "Did he say anything else to you?" How could he? His mother, the wife, and some other woman was out there but then when I was backing out my yard we looked at each other and I could tell the way his mouth was moving he was telling me he will call me later. "I wish I could have been at your house when this shit took place." I was a mad bitch too girl. "I know you was. I thought she wasn't coming to the weekend?" That's what he told me. "You know what Shekela how you know the mother didn't call and tell the heifer something." It dawn on me because she told me she had something for my ass I guess that's my surprise she called and told the wife now she is here. "I can't wait to see what's gone happen next." Me and you both. He know I'm pissed. "But you know what Shekela if she called that man wife and told her something she wrong for that she is out of line. That might be her son but she need to stay her ass in a mama's place."

Antonio was upstairs pacing the floor trying to come up with an excuse to get out the house. The house phone rung his mother picked up. "Hey there Mrs. Jackson." How you doing? "I'm doing pretty good this Dr. McGee is Antonio there?" Yes he is hold on a minute. She went upstairs and got Antonio there is a Dr. McGee on the phone. He goes downstairs pick the phone up "Antonio we have an emergency at the hospital." Say no more I'm on my way. His wife looked "What's wrong?" I don't know they just told me to get there it's an emergency. "How long you gone be gone?" I don't know. Antonio rushes and grabs his keys and headed out the door. After he got around the corner from the house he quickly grabbed his cellphone. My phone rung. Damn Kiera this Antonio right here. Hello. "I know you mad at me but please don't be baby I didn't have no idea she was coming home today." Where you at now? "On my way to the hospital it an emergency I don't what's going on. Where you at?" I'm at Kiera house. "Stay there and I'm gone call you back later OK." Aite.

"What he say?" He told me to stay here and he will call me later.

When he got to the hospital he had to preform emergency surgery. It lasted about three hours. I looked at my watch damn girl it's eleven forty five and he ain't called me back yet. He called home his wife answered the phone. Baby I'm gone be here for a while. "What's going on." I had to do a surgery and I need to stay here and make sure everything goes OK. "Do you know how long you gone be there?" No I don't go head on and go to bed and I will see you when I get home. "OK."

My phone rung "Are you still at Kiera?" Yes I am. "Come to the hospital and come to my office if I'm not there wait on me." Aite.

"Where you finna go?" He told me to come to the hospital and meet him in his office. "Well you be careful Shekela." Alright I will see you tomorrow girl. After I left her house I headed to the hospital. When I made it to his office he wasn't there. So I waited on him. About ten minutes later he walked through the door. "I'm so sorry about our special night." It's OK you didn't know she was coming. "You just don't know how bad I was trying find an excuse to get out the house to call you and talk to you. I was loosing my mind." Who is the other girl she was with? "That's her sister Brenda." You should have seen the look they gave me. "I already know baby." Why don't you just go home to your wife. "I don't want to go home to her right now I want to spend some time with you." You not gone be able to do that right now she's there waiting on you. "I told her I was gone be at the hospital for a while." He started kissing me I pulled back. "What's wrong?" You can not go home smelling like sex. "So now you don't want to give me any?" You know that's not it. "Well don't pull away from me let me do this." We started kissing. I think you may want to lock your door before somebody walk in. "Damn you are right." He grabbed me and pushed me to the door got on his knees started licking me between my thighs. "Damn your pussy smell good and I ain't even got to it yet." He pulled my shorts down. "Damn baby you ain't even got no underwear on." I grabbed the back of his head and pushed it into my pussy. I started moaning damn Antonio I missed this. I through my legs on his shoulder he pushed me up to the door. My ass was sitting in his hands as he was eating the shit out that fat ass pussy. "Oh we oh baby this pussy taste so damn good." That's it baby eat that pussy that's it eat this pussy Antonio. I felt his tongue licking me in the crack of my ass. I skeet cum all his mouth he quickly got up and placed his tongue in my mouth. I was licking to cum off his tongue he quickly turned me over. "Damn we ain't got no condoms." We don't have to do this. "Aw hell no I got to tap this ass before I go home." He pulled out his dick started rubbing the head of his dick between my pussy lips. He started pushing the head deeper into my pussy. We both started moaning. "That's it baby slap this ass on my dick." He begin to fuck me harder and harder. We both got loud. Damn Antonio we got to calm down baby we are in a hospital remember. "I know but damn this pussy so good I'm bout to nut." Come on baby that's it nut in this pussy." You want me to nut in it?" Yes come on Antonio nut in your pussy baby come on there you go nut. "Oh Shekela oh girl he it come." Come on baby let it go. He exploded all in this pussy. "Damn girl." He pulled his dick out. "Look at all that cum on my dick and balls." I turned around and drop down to my knees and lick that dick suck that dick until it got hard again. He started bouncing my head up and down. "That's it baby suck this dick." I was sucking dick and licking balls at the same time. "Girl you got skills like no other woman I know." He was fucking my mouth so hard I started gagging and choking on the dick. But I never once stop sucking that dick. I felt his hot cum dripping all down on my face. "Oh Jesus oh girl that's it suck this dick damn." After every thing was over we went into the bathroom and cleaned up. "I show don't want to go home but I know I got to. I want to spend the rest of the night with you." I know you do but go head and go home to your wife. "I can't stop thinking about you." That makes two of us. "I'm gone check on my patient and I'm gone head to the house. What is you finna do?" Go home and take a hot bubble bath. "I want to tell you something Shekela." What's that? "I have never and I repeat never felt this way about no other woman." What about your wife? "Not even her. That might sound selfish as hell but I am falling deeply in love with you and I don't know what to do about it." How do you know you are falling in love? "The way you make me feel the way my eyes light up when I see your face. I get jealous as hell when I see another man talking to you in the bedroom department baby girl you got the shit down pack to the tee. I ain't never felt this way no woman has never made me cum like you do. I ain't never even had my dick suck like that and you think your ass ain't got me crazy. You do. You are every man fantasy and more. I don't know how I'm gone do this with us living next door but I'm gone find a way to be with you and see you outside this job." I want to be with you as well I want to see you when I want to see you pick up the phone text you when I want to but I know that can't happen all I would be to you is the other woman, and I want so much more than that Antonio. "I don't look at you as the other woman." So what you call it? "A man who fell in love with his next door neighbor and want to be with her. I know this shit can't be easy for you but only if you knew how hard this shit is for me. You know what Shekela it's amazing how you knock me off my feet. Every time I get around you I get weak and no woman has ever made me feel that way. And every time you kiss me and make love to me it only make me weak for you." I don't want you to be weak for me. I'm not saying it's a bad thing I love the way you make me feel. You know what Antonio you do the same thing to me you just don't know it. I am so fortunate to have you in my life even though I'm just the girl next door. "You are so much more than just that and you know you are. I just want to make you happy from the bottom of my heart." You make me happy more than you would ever know only if you knew how much I want to be with you. I know you got rounds to make I'm gone let you go so I can go home. "You just don't know how bad I want to go home with you." I looked at him. We kissed each other goodbye. "I'll see you later beautiful." OK.

Chapter 7

When I made it home I took a hot bubble bath. Sitting there thinking about what we said to one another. My phone rung it was my sister. "How you doing?" I'm doing OK and you. "I'm concerned about you." Why? "Kiera called me and told me what happened." I'm OK I was gone call you later on and tell you about it. "Have you seen Antonio?" Yeah I just left him about twenty minutes ago. "Where bout?" He was the hospital and he called and told me to come up there see him and I did. "So tell me what the wife look like?" She alright. "She just alright?" She is an average looking wife. "Are you still going to see Antonio?" I sure am. "How is that possible and he live right next door?" When there is a will there is a way. "I just don't want you to give your hopes up to high and you get hurt in the end because ain't nothing good gone come out of this messing around with a married man." I hear what you saying but you or nobody else is going to tell me otherwise I'm going to continue to see Antonio. "OK." I want us to get together Saturday and have a barbecue at my house. "A barbecue?" Yes we will invite a few friends and have a get together in the back yard. "Honestly I'm kind of anxious to see what the wife look like." I told you. "Did she give you a fucked up look?" Now you know she did especially when he introduce us. I think his mama had something to do with that. "Why?" The old bat told me she had a surprise for me and I guess this was it the wife is here like that is gone stop me from getting what I want. Let me get through taking a bath so I can go to bed and I will talk to you tomorrow. "Shekela you take care of your self alright." I will.

When he made it home everybody in the house was sleep he went upstairs and got in the shower. When he finished he got in the bed she turn over and wrap her arms around him. Damn I show hope she don't want no sex tonight because I am wore out. "You just getting in?" Yes I am. "I miss you." I miss you too but I am so tired. "Too tired to make love to your wife?" Honestly yes I am. "You never been too tired to make love to me." It's not that I don't want to make love to you. "What are you saying then?" I'm just tired. "What about you just lay there and I do all the work." If that is what you wanna do. She climbed on top of him started kissing him. He closed his eyes thinking to his self woman I wish you would just roll over and go to bed, because this woman just fuck me and suck my dick so good I doubt if my dick even get up. I guess I better get on up and fuck her so she won't think nothing is going on. I will fuck her so she can get a nut and turn around and go to sleep because I'm dead tired the only thing on my mind right now is that woman next door wondering what she doing right now. After they got done fucking he turned over and went to sleep.

Over the next few days his wife couldn't do nothing but look at me every time she seen me she didn't speak but she gave me a fucked up look like she wanted to say something to me. The only time me and Antonio seen each other was when we was at work. When he was at home he barely came outside but we text each other quite often to let each other know we was missing one another.

I called everyone to let them know I was having a barbecue at my house Saturday at three o'clock. Everybody was down for that. It was Saturday morning about ten o'clock I got up and started getting everything together. I got an text from Antonio to let me know he was getting ready to take his mom to the airport. I smiled it's about damn time her nosy ass go home. I text him back I hope I get a chance to see you later, if I don't call me. He respond to my text I'm gone try my best to get out the house tonight so I can see you.

My door bell rung it was Chris bringing the barbecue grill over. "Don't worry about buying any meat I got everything." I appreciate that big brother. "So what you finna do now?" I'm finna go to the store and buy everything else. As I was outside talking to Chris Antonio mom came outside. She just looked at me with a smile on her face. "Well I'll be back later on to start barbecuing." OK Chris. I went back in the house and grabbed my purse and my keys. When I came back out I seen Antonio bringing the suitcase out the house. He smiled at me I smiled back. Moments later the wife and the kids came behind him.

Kiera showed up. "Where you finna go?" To the store. "Well I'm gone ride with you." We got in my truck. "Is that the wife?" Yes that's her. "Damn she is plan Jane as fine as Antonio is and he with her." We left my house heading to the grocery store. He sent me a text this morning and told me he was taking his mom to the airport. "She taking her nosy ass home." Yes indeed. "I know you glad she going home so she can get the fuck out y'all business." You have no idea how happy I am. "All you got to do is worry about the wife." Trust me she is not a problem. "So when you gone see Antonio again." We gone try to hook up tonight.

When we got to the store we started getting the food. "Damn Shekela that sexy man looking at you." He started walking toward us. "Well hey ladies." Hey how you doing? "What's your name?" Shekela. "Well Shekela I'm Tyrese." Well hey Tyrese. "You look like somebody I know." Is that a good thing or a bad thing? "It's a good thing." This is my best friend Kiera. "Well hey there." Hey. "Look like somebody finna do some serious cooking." We getting ready to have a barbecue at my house. "Am I invited?" I laughed at him. Do you want to come. "Only if you invite me." Well here is my number and you call me if you want to come. "Do you have a boyfriend." Yes. "I bet not come then I might want to take you away from him." Kiera started laughing. "Well if I don't come to the barbecue I'm definitely gone call you." He walked off.

"Damn Shekela." He is sexy. "What about the doctor?" I looked at Kiera and started laughing I just said the brother was sexy. "Then you gone give him your phone number." Well he said he wanted to come to the barbecue. "You gone make Antonio act a fool." Ain't nothing wrong with two men fighting over a woman. "You right but somebody can get hurt." You know what they say let the best man win. "Girl you wrong for that one." Girl I'm just having some fun I ain't trying to fuck him. I'm trying to give this pussy to Antonio. "Well hell let me fuck him he fine as shit." You can have him. Kiera said "Ain't that Alexandria. What is you doing in the store?" Getting some stuff for the barbecue I tired to call you. "You ain't called my cell phone." No I called your house phone. "Well we in the store doing the same thing. Alexandria let me tell you girl. "What?" I seen Antonio wife. "What do she look like?" All I'm gone say Shekela ain't got no competition. "Damn she that jacked up?" We all started laughing. She look alright. "So Shekela have you seen or been with Antonio?" I seen him today and I was with him a couple of nights ago at his office. "Damn y'all fucking at the hospital." Girl we tore that shit up. "Where was the wife?" At home, and his mama is going home today. "I know you excited." You have no ideal. Lets finish shopping because I got a lot of stuff to do at the house before the party kick off. "Well I'm gone go home and cook the stuff I bought and I will see y'all later." OK.

After we finished shopping we headed back to my house and started getting everything together. We put some music on Kiera made some drinks. My sister showed up. What's this? "I bought some stuff for the party too." You didn't have to we bought everything. "I wanted to help." Well that's fine we finna start cooking so come on. Grab an apron girlfriend.

Tekela I seen Antonio wife today. "Where bout?" Outside. "Did she speak?" You know damn well that girl wasn't gone speak to me. "I don't know why not you ain't fucking her husband no offense Shekela." Well hell none taken. We all started laughing. About an hour and a half later Chris showed up and start barbecuing. When Anthony got there he started deep frying the fish. We was outside getting everything set up. Kiera said "Did you invite Dr. McGee?" I sure did. Y'all take care of everything outside I'ma go in the house take a bath and put some clothes on. "You already got some clothes on." Girl please now you know I got to look sexy.

After I step out the shower I did my hair and makeup, went into my closet door to find something to put on. As I was searching for something to wear I found this hot pink sun dress with all the back out sexy as hell. Reached into the top of my closet and pulled out my hot pink stilettos. As I was getting ready Antonio and his wife showed up. She looked at him. "I guess our neighbor having a party." I guess so. Alexandria and her baby daddy showed up. After I finished getting dressed I went downstairs. Chris and Anthony looked at me "Damn who you getting all dressed up for?" Nobody. When I walked outside to the backyard everybody looked at me. Damn why is all eyes on me? "You had to get dressed up and put on stilettos to have a barbecue?" Is it anything wrong with looking sexy? "No it's not."

She looked at Antonio "Well since our neighbor having a big barbecue lets take the kids out and do something." Well I'm actually on call the hospital can call me at any given time. Why don't you and Brenda take the kids to the movies, or skating or to the park. "What are you going to do?" I'm gone get some sleep. "Well I would like for us to do something as a family." We will.

Kiera said "Alexandria come here hurry up. That's the doctor wife." Ewwww that's her. "Yup."

Brenda said "Antonio isn't going?" No he say he gone stay home and get some rest he's on call. "I need to be at that party." Why? "Girl don't you see all them good men coming in and out?"

Me and my sister went out to my truck to get the pops. "Damn Mariah look it's two of them." Girl they twins. "Antonio didn't tell you she had a twin sister." No he didn't. "Girl that's some scary shit they look identical alike. You can tell the different between both of them." Why you say that? "Look what the hoe got on." They started laughing.

Don't look Tekela but Antonio wife is looking at us. "Well can I turn around I want to see her." Slowly turn around and look. She on the driver side. "She look OK." You said the right word OK.

"Mommy is daddy coming with us?" No he is not baby. "Where are we going?" What y'all want to do? "We want to go to the park." OK that is what we gone do take y'all to the park.

After they left Antonio was standing in front of the window watching everything that's going on. Damn look at my baby. She look sexy as hell in pink. Dr. McGee just showed up. I know she did not invite him.

When they got to the park the kids start running around and playing. "Mariah let me ask you something?" Whats that? "Do you think Antonio sleeping with her?" No I don't. Do she want to fuck him? Yes. He is not the cheating type. I know I might sound crazy for saying that but I don't think my husband will cheat on me with another woman he's about family. As hard as we tried to keep this thing together maintain I don't think he will fuck that up. But I will tell you one thing Brenda if she think for one minute I'm gone let her come in our family take my husband and my kids father away from them she got another thing coming. She may be glamours, long hair, nice body, pretty face but that hoe will not take my husband away from me. "I hear what you saying and I don't blame you fight for whats yours. You want a lil bit of advise?" What's that? "Step your game up girl." What do you mean? "I'm not telling you to dress like a hoe want you start dressing sexy keep his attention, put on some makeup, wear something sexy to bed sometime. I'm not saying you in competition with her but think about it no man wants a boring unattractive wife. I'm not saying that's you but when you live next door to somebody like her you gone have to keep your game tight." I see where you coming from but Antonio married me for me not for what I look like. "That may be so but look at your competition is." Any other time if you would have asked Antonio to come with you and y'all have a family day he would have came." You right he would have. "I'm not saying Antonio is cheating because I don't think he is he doesn't seem like he that type of brother who would cheat on his wife. But never underestimate a man because you are not with him twenty four hours a day seven days a week. You don't know what's going through his mind but you got to understand one thing." And what's that? "He is still a man."

The barbecue was off the hook. Dr. McGee just pulled up. Antonio is looking out the window.

Damn she is having a party and she ain't even tell me. And look at my baby looking so sexy in pink. Them pink stilettos on all she doing right now is turning me the fuck on. I know that can't be him Dr. McGee hugging my woman where is my cellphone let me send her ass a text. So you having a party you didn't invite me then you gone let Dr. McGee hug you on top of all that. Text me back.

Me and Kiera went inside the house and start bringing more food out. I checked my phone he sent me a text let me text him back. I'm sorry I didn't tell you about the party I know you couldn't come so really it wasn't no point of telling you. Yes I invited Dr. McGee we all work together I hope you like my outfit I'm wearing this just for you. He quickly replied back "You know I'm watching you. You have no idea how bad I want to kiss you don't you dare let Dr. McGee rub my ass cheeks." I text back you know that's not gone happen these cheeks belong to you. Is it possible for you to come next door to get a plate? "As bad as I want to I can't I don't know when she will be back." That's understandable I will just put you a plate up for later if we get a chance to hook up. He replied "OK sexy but I am watching you I just want you to know that." I laughed and I went back outside and join the party.

They got the kids together and they stop by and picked up pizza and headed home. Brenda do you mind getting the table together I'm gone go upstairs to see if Antonio hungry. He heard her coming up the steps he jumped in bed and pretended like he was sleep. She walked in the room and sat on side of the bed. Antonio are you asleep I bought pizza home are you hungry? "Um just a little bit." How could you sleep with all that noise going on outside. "If you tired like me you will sleep through all of that." Can I ask you a question? "What's that?" Did you know Shekela had an identical twin sister. I just looked at her. "Yes I knew." How did you know? "We all work together at the hospital." You didn't tell me that. "That was nothing to tell she is our neighbor and we work at the hospital together. What's up with all the questions about our neighbor?" I'm not asking a lot of questions about her we gone be living next door to one another we might as well get to know each other maybe we can become friends. "I'm surprise you said that." Why? "If I recall you don't like to hang around a lot of women." I don't but she seems like a nice person. "Well lets go downstairs and eat so I can come back and go to sleep. Damn why is she asking a lot of questions about our neighbor I wonder have my mother talked to her. Nawl she wouldn't never turn on me she wouldn't tell her what's going on what she think is going on. Then again I don't know she didn't suppose to come her until Saturday. I'm her favorite son she wouldn't never do that to me."

It's about eight o'clock the party is whining down people are starting to leave. Me, Kiera, Tekela, and Alexandria we started cleaning up. I went to check my phone and he left me a text message. I sent him a text to see was he gone be able to get out the house tonight. After I did that we started putting the food up.

When his dad came home from work his mom sat him down and talked to him. You may want to have a talk with Antonio. "About what?" I think he may be cheating on Mariah. "Are you serious with who?" His next door neighbor. "Antonio will not do something like that he is not that type of man." I know that and you know that but if you seen his next door neighbor you would think otherwise. "Tell me why do you think our son is cheating?" The way they look at one another every time she see him she half ass naked. Can you believe he went out one night stayed out all night and wouldn't answer his cellphone and didn't come home till the next morning. "Well maybe he was out with some friends." Let me refresh your memory. Remember when you was with your first wife that's the same thing you told her when you was cheating with me. "What do she look like?" She is beautiful and we both know Antonio and Mariah already having problems they don't need no drama like that going on. "I understand where you coming from baby but Antonio is a grown man if you want me to I will have a talk with him but that's all I can do is talk to him." Well I'm not gone stand by and watch someone hurt my family. "I think you may be reading to much into this. I know women like her she look like she a home wrecker. To ease your mind I'm off for a couple of days I will go to Atlanta spend sometime with him and talk to him." That's a good idea and when you talk to him remind him that he have a wife, a family, and a career. "I can remind him all those things but at the end of the day Antonio is still gone do what Antonio want to do." Take his brother Pete with him and y'all can talk to him together. "Maybe he don't want his brother knowing his business and to be honest he might not want me to know his business." Well somebody got to do something cause my son and your son is thinking with the wrong head.

After we finished putting the food up and cleaning up me and the girls sat around and talked for a while. Kiera said "Do you think you gone see Antonio tonight?" I don't know I sent him a text he haven't respond to it. My sister reply "Maybe he can't get out the house the wife could have him on lock down." That may be true but if a man want to get out and play trust and believe me he will find a way. Alexandria laughed "She is right if Antonio wants to get out he will get out. So what are you finna do?" I'm gone take a shower and I'm gone get dressed cause I got a feeling I'm gone see Antonio. "Well get ready and go home and if you don't see Antonio call us and we'll get together and go out to the club somewhere." I will keep that in mind.

It was about ten o'clock after they left I went upstairs and took a hot shower and got dressed and waited on Antonio to send me a text. I got a text "Meet me at the hospital in my office go head on and leave first."

After she finished giving the kids a bath she put them to bed. She went upstairs. What are you doing? "I'm looking for my folders I need them." Folders for what? "I got some important papers in there and I need them." Are you sure you bought them home? "I thought I did I'm gone have to go to my office." Can't you wait until tomorrow? "No I need those papers. And I also need to check on two of my patients as well." Do you want me to wait up for you. "You can if you want to."

After he left he called me "Where are you?" About five minutes away from the hospital. "I'm on my way."

She went downstairs and sat on the couch Brenda sat next to her. Are you OK? "Honestly I don't know. Where is Antonio?" He say he gone to the hospital to get some papers he need. "At this time of the night he couldn't wait until tomorrow." That's the same thing I said he said it is important though. "Do you believe him?" I guess I do. "Nawl Mariah that's not what I asked you do you believe he gone to the hospital." Yeah I believe him. "You don't sound like you are convinced let me look out the window and see if her truck gone. What a coincidence her truck gone and he just left." That doesn't mean anything Brenda. "The only way you gone have a peace of mind you gone have to talk to Antonio if you suspects he cheating ask him." I'm not gone ask him that. "And why not?" I'm not gone give him the benefit of the doubt that I am insecure about our marriage. "That doesn't make you insecure Mariah." Can we change the subject I'm going upstairs and go to bed. "If you want to talk I'm here." I appreciate that.

When he made it to the hospital I was in his office waiting on him. He rushed in and quickly locked the door he picked me up and laid me on top of his desk pulled down his pants put a condom on and put my legs over his shoulder and rushed his dick inside my tight pussy. We started kissing moaning. "I can't stay long but I got to have this pussy before I go to bed." I took off my shirt. He started biting on my nipples he flipped my ass over and hit that shit from the back. He was pounding that pussy so hard I was throwing everything on the floor off his desk. I bounced up and down on that dick the harder he fuck me pussy juice was going everywhere hitting him all in his chest and face pussy was so wet. His dick kept coming out of it. He was moaning his ass off. "I'm finna get this nut." He quickly pulls his dick out the pussy take the condom off and he skeet all over my ass and my back. Calling my name. When we finished he was breathing hard as hell. "Damn baby that shit was so good I couldn't wait to put my dick in you." He grabbed my face and we started kissing. "I gotta get cleaned up so I can get back to the house I hate to make love to you and leave." It's all good this is what we call a quickie it was worth the wait though. We went into the bathroom and got cleaned up. "Did you have fun at your barbecue?" We had a good time. "I know you did I watched you all day until she came home. You have no idea how bad I wanted to come make love to you with that hot pink dress on. Pink stilettos my dick been hot all day for you. You ain't gone believe this shit my wife asked me questions about you today." What kind of questions? "I guess she seen you and Tekela outside and ask me did I know you had a twin sister I told her yes. She asked me how did I know I told her we all walk together at the hospital she said you seem like a nice person since y'all neighbors maybe y'all can become friends." I started laughing yeah right me and her friends and I'm fucking her husband OK. "But baby I'm gone grab these papers so I can go home I don't want to but I got to and I will talk to you later." OK. We hugged and kissed goodbye.

After I left the hospital I went home and got in the bed. When he got home he went to bed. She turned over "Did you get your papers?" Yes I got everything I need. She got up went downstairs and looked out the window. "He just getting home she's at home. Could this be a coincidence or could they be fucking? Could he really cheat on me? I'm his wife we have kids together." She goes back to stairs and get in the bed just looked at him thinking to her self. "I hope and pray you are not cheating on me that will hurt me so bad and if you are I will fucking hurt you." She closed her eyes and went to sleep.

Chapter 8

It's Monday morning about five o'clock time to get up and go to work. I didn't see Antonio all yesterday that concerned me wondering why he didn't text me or call. After I got up and got my day started I grabbed some breakfast and headed to work.

Soon as I walked in the door I bumped right into my sister. "We didn't hear from you yesterday." I was tired I slept all day yesterday. "So did you see Antonio Saturday night?" I sure did. "How did he manage that?" I told you when there is a will there is a way. "Did he stay out all night?" No. "Well I'm gone talk to you later I got some work I got to do."

Today has been a very busy day for me. It was about two forty five I just got an text from Antonio. "I been in surgery all day that's why I haven't had a chance to call you or text you. I'm also sorry about yesterday I didn't get a chance to talk to you." After I got off work I went to the gym to get my workout on. After I left I went home took a shower went to the beauty shop to get my hair done.

It was about six o'clock in the afternoon Antonio was just making it home. Damn this look like my dad car in the drive way. When he walked in the door his dad and brother was sitting on the couch playing with the kids and talking to his wife. Hey dad and Pete what are y'all doing here. "We come to spend a little time with you if that's OK." That's fine by me. When did y'all get in town. "About an hour and half ago we wanted to surprise you." Well you did that. "Me and Brenda and the kids gone go to the store to get groceries so I can come back and cook dinner for everybody."

"So gone and tell your daddy how you like Atlanta?" I love it Atlanta is beautiful. "And your new job?" It's good. "So big brother you making more money too huh?" Yeah the money is even better. Well come on dad y'all lets go outside and sit on the porch it's a nice day outside. So why y'all didn't tell me y'all was coming to Atlanta? "I got a few days off I needed a vacation your mom told me Atlanta is beautiful and she was right and I wanted to come see what was going on with my son." I'm good day and Pete I can't believe you came. "I needed some time off too and you know dad he don't like to go nowhere by his self." They all started laughing. "So son your mama told me about your neighbor." Oh dad don't tell me that is why you came to Atlanta because you listen to what mom told you. "That's not what it is son. I'm not listening to anything I'm here to talk to you." There is nothing to talk about mom is jumping through all the conclusions. She is my neighbor my friend we work together and that is that. "You know your mother you know how over protected she is and she is just worried about you." But I'm OK. "Look Antonio I'm your father this is your brother whatever we discuss right here it stays between the three of us. You can talk to me about anything. So what is her name?" Who? "Your neighbor." Her name is Shekela, she is a nurse we work at the same hospital she got an identical twin sister she is a very nice young lady. "I heard she is pretty." She is. She is very attractive. Pete said "Is she single?" Leave it along Pete. "Well your mama told me every time y'all see one another y'all give each other eye contact is it true?" Mom is reading to much in to this. "You can talk to me I'm not gone tell your mother what we talk about I never do because I know how your mom is." "Wait a minute dad. Antonio why you gone tell me to leave it alone is she single?" Yes she is. As they was on the porch talking I drove up. Don't look now but there she go. When I got out my truck "Hey Shekela." Hey Antonio. "This is my father and my brother Peter." Hey y'all. "Hey how you doing?" I'm doing good. "My dad and my brother is here for a couple of days." OK I hope you guys enjoy Atlanta. "It was nice meeting you Shekela." It was nice meeting you guys.

I walked in the house. "Damn son that's your neighbor?" That's her. Antonio looked at his brother you may want to pick up your bottom lip and close your mouth. "I think I'm in love." Pete leave that alone. "Son why is you keep telling your brother to leave that alone if nothing is going on between you and her. Is it something you want to tell us?" OK dad I'm attractive to her. "Well son you're only human she a fine ass woman. Don't tell your mother I said that." They laughed. "Are y'all sleeping together?" Antonio just looked. "You just answered the question. You ain't even got to tell me." Pete said "You lucky ass man." Why you say that? "You sleeping with something that fine." Between the three of us dad I'm falling in love with her. "Oh shit do your wife have any idea?" No she don't. "So what are you going to do?" I don't know I love my wife. "Did she put the pussy on you that good?" Dad, Pete I ain't never had a woman to do the things that woman do to me. She got my mind all fucked up. "Is she a freak?" Pete when I tell you she is a freak she is a super freak. It's not just about the sex with her I'm falling in love with her for who she is on the inside as well as the outside. When I moved to Atlanta I had no idea that I was gone end up falling in love with my next door neighbor. And the things she do to me it blows my mind away. "What do she do tell us." Nawl Pete it's just some things a man keep to his self. "You're right son don't tell us all your personal business but she is fine." I go to bed thinking about her I wake up she is on my mind. Every time I see her talking to another man I get jealous it's another doctor at the hospital I work at he like her and it burns me up every time I see him in her face. "Damn son you do got it bad." Dad please don't say nothing to mom. "I promise you we're not gone say anything this is between the three of us like I told you. But you need to figure out what you want to do and who you want to be with." I know I'm wrong dad for cheating on my wife. "I'm not here to judge you Antonio because I been there I know what you going through."

When I made it in the house I started cleaning up. I gathered all the trash together so I can take it outside. Let me change clothes because I know Antonio gone look. I went upstairs put on some tight ass jeans and a half t-shirt. I went outside dumped the trash in the garbage went into my truck pretending I was looking for something.

"Damn son she got some ass on her. Oh my bad son." He looked at his dad and laughed.

I slowly walked back into the house and closed the door.

"I see why you in love if I was living next door to a woman like that I probably would be in love too son." Dad let me ask you a question it would be wrong for me to leave my wife and kids won't it? "I can't tell you that you have to follow your heart. It's not about what I say, your brother say, your mother say, nobody say. Antonio got to do what makes him happy." She makes me happy. But I don't want to hurt Mariah and my kids. Peter said "Antonio how long y'all been sleeping together?" You won't believe this shit the first day I moved here. "Damn!" She turned me out. Only if you guys knew the things she did to me. "Are you gone tell us?" No. I'll be right back dad I got to go used the bathroom. He went into the house grabbed his cellphone "You know you was wrong for coming outside with them tight ass jeans on girl you got my dick hard. Can you believe it I'm telling my dad and my brother all about me and you I love you Shekela." I got his text I text him back I love you too Antonio and that is very sweet of you to tell your dad and brother about us. I put them jeans on just for you to watch my ass smile. "Believe me I couldn't take my eyes off you even my dad had to say damn. My brother asked me did you have a boyfriend so I had to come clean and tell them the truth then because my brother will not get his hands on you. I will talk to you later beautiful." After I read that text I smiled I'm crazy about that man.

Over the next few days I didn't see much of him he was spending time with his dad and brother. About a week later his wife started to dress a little sexy I seen her one day I started laughing I thought the shit was funny now she want to seduce her husband. She should have been taking care of her home long time ago before he met a woman like me who turned his whole world upside down.

Three months has past by me and Antonio are still seeing each other. His wife is starting to get suspicious because Antonio is never where he suppose to be. He sent me a text and asked me could I take a couple of days off from work and go to New York with him on a doctor convention. I text him back and said yes what about your wife. "I told her she couldn't go because I would be very busy."

When we got to New York we had candle light dinners, long walks in the park, and we did a carriage ride. In three days we made love, we had sex, and we fucked like two dogs in heat. I felt like I was in paradise. A couple other nurses at the hospital started rumors that me and Antonio was involved. His wife started asking questions, and she found out that I was out of town as well. It was a Friday afternoon we had just got back in town. I had Kiera to pick me up at the airport. Antonio told me he was finna go to the house and he was gone talk to me later. When he got home she was in the living room on the couch with tears in her eyes. What's wrong is everything OK? She looked at him "How was your vacation?" It was good why is you sitting in the dark crying? "I got a lot of stuff on my mind." Where the kids? "They went to Dallas with Brenda for a couple of days. Did you and your girlfriend enjoy your vacation in New York?" He looked excuse me? "You heard me I know all about you and the hoe next door." I don't know what you heard but it is not true. "Antonio how could you look me in the face and tell me a bald face lie like you ain't fucking that girl!" Shekela there is nothing going on. "I can't believe this shit I'm gone ask you one more time for the truth and if don't tell it to me you gone see another side of me you never seen before. Now I'm gone ask your lying ass one more time. How long you been fucking her?" Let me explain it to you. "I don't want your sorry ass to explain a damn thing to me! Answer the fucking question!" We been sleeping together since the first night I got to Atlanta. "The first night you fuck this bitch on the first night you moved here? You trifling ass dog. How could you do this to me and your family?" Are you gone let me explain it to you. Tears start rolling down here face. Mariah I promise I never meant to hurt you. "You hurt me the day you stuck your dick in her! Do you love her and tell me the fucking truth!" I don't think you want me to answer that question. She got up off the couch and slapped the living hell out of him. "Now I'm gone ask your bitch ass one more time do you love this hoe?" Yes I do. "You got to be fucking joking me." She started hitting him in the face with her fist hollering and screaming "How could you do this to me!" I'm sorry. "Your ass ain't sorry you sorry cause your ass got caught. All them late nights you wasn't coming home you was with her." Yes. "You trifling ass dog. Tell me Antonio I'm not pretty enough for you I don't have long hair, I'm not light skin with a big ass. Is that what it is?" No that is not what it is at all. "Well tell me what it is about her that made you fall in love with her." Her personality she is very sweet she listen to me she understands me. "You mean to tell me I don't listen to you?" Not like her. "You got to be joking me. I gave you two kids we took wedding vows together. So you didn't take that shit serious at all." We been having problems with our marriage way before I got involved with Shekela. "What did you tell me you told me when we moved we gone start first new and make this marriage work for the sake of our kids." I thought that was what I wanted. "So what are you saying you want out of this marriage?" Honestly I don't know what I want. "Antonio if you don't stop telling me this bullshit and be honest with me I'm gone go upside your motherfucking head. I sat here on this couch for the last couple of days thinking about all those nights you wasn't at home. You had to run to the store to get something, you always forgot something, and every time you left she was never at home so evidently you was going to meet her. Am I right or wrong?" You're right. "Did you even use a condom with the bitch?" Sometimes. "Sometimes? You mean to tell me your dumb ass didn't wrap up your dick every time you fucked her." No. "You a stupid motherfucker. If you fuck up and bring a disease home you are a dead man." She don't sleep around like that. "How you know what this hoe ain't doing. If she fuck you on the first night you think she won't fuck another man on the first night." She's not that type of woman. "You mean to tell me you gone stand here in my face and defend this bitch. All those nights I wanted to make love to you what did you tell me I'm tired, I'm sleepy, I don't feel like it, I got an headache. And all those times you was out fucking her. But you know what Antonio you better break shit off with that hoe because if you don't I'm gone make your life a living hell." What do you mean you gone make my life a living hell? "I will fix it so you want see your kids and put your ass on child support." You can't take my kids away from me. "Watch me and see. Test me and find out. Now you tell me who it's going to be your family or the bitch next door." You know I love my kids and I will do anything in the world for them. "Well if you love your kids you better end this shit right now with her." I'm sorry I can't do that I'm in love with her. "You know what then since you love her so much you just lost your kids." You can't do that to me. "Watch me and see you fucked this marriage up by yourself."

Me and Kiera just pulled up in my drive way laughing and talking. His wife come storming out the door. "You nasty ass bitch!" Excuse me? "You heard what I said hoe. I found out about you fucking my husband." Antonio came outside "Mariah come on quit making a scene outside. "You gone tell me to quit making a scene and you fucking this trifling ass bitch." Antonio you better get your wife before she get a fucking beat down. "Nawl bitch come on because you know what you deserve to get your ass kick for fucking with somebody else man." She ran up on me I hit her dead in her fucking face. We got the fighting. Antonio and Kiera was trying to break the fight up. But me and that hoe was going at it. They finally pull us apart. "Bitch I hate you!" Well you know what your husband love me. "Come on in the house Mariah." "Come on Shekela lets go in the house." Everybody in the neighborhood was outside. "You mean to tell me that's the kind of hoe you want for a woman?" Mariah you went outside and you started that fight.

"If you defend this hoe one more time me and you gone be fighting next." Would you calm down now sit down let me go get an ice pack for your face.

"Damn Shekela you beat the hell out that girl." She fucking with the wrong one. I'm glad all this shit is out in the open so me and Antonio ain't got to sneak and duck and hide no fucking more. That bitch done pissed me off and up set my fucking nerves.

Mariah would you just calm down. "Antonio please tell me you not finna walk away from our family please. Think about your kids think about what is this doing to me." I'm sorry I never meant to hurt you. "If you don't want to hurt me don't leave us let her go. I will do anything for you just don't leave us." Antonio started crying. "Tell me Antonio do you love me?" Yes I love you. "Do you love your kids?" More than anything in this world you know I do. "Well if you love us don't leave us. Please. We are nothing without you. I can't do this without you. Our kids need their father I need my husband my soul mate. I been in love with you for so long. I'm nothing without you Antonio you can't leave me I won't let you. Think about what this gone do to our kids if you walk away and leave us. I'm begging you please don't go." All he could do is look at her.

Kiera called my sister and Alexandria and told them to come over to the house me and Antonio wife just got the fighting. My sister and Alexandria showed up. "What the hell happened over here?" Kiera said "Girl the wife know about them and she come storming out that door in Shekela face I ain't even gone lie Shekela beat the brakes off her ass. Me and Antonio had to pull them apart. "Are you OK Shekela?" I'm fine. My sister looked at me "I knew this was gone happen somebody was gone get hurt. Shekela you got to let this man go now." That's where you wrong at Tekela I'm gone fight for what's mine. "He is not your man he belong to somebody else." When you get through talking I'm still gone fuck Antonio. "I don't want to see you get hurt. That woman know about y'all now and she gone be out for revenge." Do you think I care I'm in love with this man I'm not giving him up. Alexandria said "Tekela you can't expect Shekela to just drop this man like a bag of potatoes. She is in love with this man." "But he's not hers." "It doesn't matter Antonio love her as well." "That may be so he may love you Shekela but he got a family." I'm his family now. My sister said "Kiera please talk some sense into her she will listen to your before she will listen to me." Tekela I will have to agree with Alexandria she's in love and when a woman is in love there is nothing we can say to her to make her leave that man. Only she can walk away and leave him when she get tired. Look at your sister take a look at her she is in love. You know how love feel you been with a married man before. "Yes I have and that's why I'm telling her she got to let it go because at the end of the day he didn't choose me he chose his wife and his family." Well that's you Tekela Shekela is a different whole person. How do you know this man here won't leave his wife? "Well what if he don't?" If he don't that is something your sister got to go through she got to deal with that until that happen I'm gone stay out of it. And I think we all should stay out of this and let Shekela and Antonio deal with this situation here.

A few moments later we heard a knock on the door. Kiera open the door it was Antonio. "Hey Kiera I need to talk to Shekela in private." Shekela Antonio is at the door and he want to talk in private. "OK let him in." "Well come on ladies lets go and let them talk in private" Kiera said. My sister just looked at Antonio and rolled her eyes. They left out the door. "Sit down please we really need to talk. I am so sorry Shekela that all this happened." This is not your fault. "Yes it is because when I got involved with you I knew I was married and one day this was gone happened she was gone find out. I love you more than you will ever know Shekela I do but I love my kids as well." So what are you saying? "I'm sorry from the bottom of my heart but I got to try to make this thing work if I want to see my kids." Are you leaving me? "I don't want to." I started crying. "Please don't cry baby." You told me you love me and you want to be with me. "I do." So why are you doing this to us? "I'm not doing this to hurt you." So you choose your wife over me? "I choose my kids." You can raise those kids without being with your wife. "She is the mother of my kids and I owe her that much to try to make this thing work." Well you know what Antonio you should have thought about that when you was fucking me. I hate you! Get the fuck out my house! "Don't do that Shekela." I don't want to see you don't text me don't call me don't even fucking look at me anymore. When you see me at work act like you don't see me. "Is this what you gone do to us?" Look what the fuck you doing to us. You choose your wife now you take your ass home to your wife. "I love you." You take that love and you shove it up your ass because every thing you told me it's been a lie. "No it hasn't. Everything I told you been the truth." Fuck you and the truth. Get the fuck up out my house. "I can not leave you being angry at me right now I need you to understand what I'm doing." Understand you? I looked at him and tears continued to run down my face. I got up and I slapped the shit out of him. "OK I deserve that." You deserve so much more you lucky I don't have a gun. "So now you want to kill me." Like I said, you're lucky. Now get your tired ass up and go home to your wife. He got up "At least let me hug and kiss you before I go." Bitch you must be out your fucking mind. "Would you do me one favor then don't go out and sleep with no one else let me try to figure out my marriage." If you think I'm gone sit around here hold my pussy on hold until you figure out who you want to be with you must be stuck on stupid. "So I guess now you gone run to Dr. McGee." And if I do you ain't got a damn thing to say about it now I can fuck who I want to fuck. "Well I tell you one thing Shekela I bet not catch you fucking nobody else." And if you do what you gone do tell your wife. You got some fucking nerves to tell me to put my pussy on hold for you. "I told you that because I love you and I'm trying to fix this." Go away and don't come back. As he was walking out the door I ran behind him started hitting him in the back I hate you I hate your mother fucking ass. He walked out and closed the door. I went into the living room and laid on the couch and cried.

When he walked in the house he looked at his wife. I did what you asked me to do. He went upstairs went into the bathroom and locked the door, sat down on the toilet and cried. Thinking to himself how could I let this woman go I love this woman. Am I doing the right thing. She make me feel like no other woman has. I love my wife but I'm in love with Shekela. I hope and pray one day she will understand why I did this. I did it because of my kids.

The next morning my phone rung for hours I didn't answer. I didn't want to talk to anyone or see anybody. When I finally got up I took a shower got something to eat check my messages and got in the bed. Antonio is at the hospital making his rounds he forgot his cell phone at home. The wife was cleaning up and ran across is phone and started going through it. She found several of pictures of me naked playing with my pussy I had sent to Antonio and started crying. She started going through his text messages as she can see we was texting each other everyday several times. She started to read some of them. He was telling me how much he love me, he miss me, and how he can't wait to make love to me. She just sat there with tears running down her face. He really do love this woman. Have I lost my husband and my kids father. What do I need to do to bring the excitement back into our bedroom.

After he finished his rounds he went to his office lock the door and sat there, thinking about everything that's going on in his life right now. They went out of town for a couple of days to try to fix the marriage but the only thing was on his mind was me. In the back of her mind she knew her marriage was over but she was still trying to hold on to him.

I took a couple of days off work to get myself together. My sister, Kiera, and Alexandria came over. I let them in. "We been calling you for days are you OK?" I'm gone be OK. My sister looked at me "He broke up with you didn't he?" Yes he did. "Shekela I am so sorry I knew this was gone happen that's why I didn't want you to get involved with him." Tekela right now I really don't want to here this. Kiera put her arms around me "I am so sorry." Alexandria said "I am too Shekela." Would y'all believe me if I told you he asked me not to fuck nobody else. "Are you serious?" Yes. Kiera said "What are you going to do now?" I'm gone pull myself together and I'm gone go back to work tomorrow and I'm gone be OK. It hurts like hell but I got to move on with my life as well. My sister said "Why don't you come stay with me for a couple of days?" No that's OK I got a house of my own. "I know you do but its going to be hard for you, y'all live right next door to one another." That might be so but I can look at his ass and act like I don't see him. If y'all could of seen the look on his face when he left here. He is hurting just as worst as I am right now. Because I know he don't love her. He told the only reason he staying with her is because of the kids. My sister said "Do you believe him?" It doesn't matter it really doesn't. If he want her he could have her.

When he made it home from the hospital she had candles lit everywhere. Romantic dinner and she even had on some sexy lingerie. He looked at her what's all this? I want to show you how much I love you. She walked up to him and started kissing him. He pulled back. "What's wrong with you?" I'm not in the mood. "What do you mean you not in the mood?" I'm tired I just want to go upstairs and laid down. "I went through all this trouble and you won't even participate." Like I said I'm tired. "But if it was the bitch next door you would have been all on her." Don't go there. "Nawl don't you go there. You left your cellphone this morning and I'm not gone lie to you yes I went through it and I seen all the naked pictures she sent you and read all the text messages when you told her you love her and miss her." You had no business going through my phone. "I'm your wife I have every right to go through your phone." No you don't just because we are married it does not give you the right to go through my phone. "Well I thought maybe we could share this day together because the kids will be home tomorrow. Are you even gone try to make this marriage work Antonio?" I did what you wanted me to do we out of town for a couple of days we came home nothing has changed. "Because you is not putting your effort into anything. You sitting around her moping looking like you lost your best friend." I have. "Fuck you!" I'm gone act like I didn't hear that. Now I'm going upstairs take a shower and lay down. "What about dinner?" I'm not hungry.

I just step out the shower and walk into my bedroom. The blinds was open I was sitting on the edge of the bed drying off. Antonio walked into their bedroom he can see me sitting on the bed drying my body off. "Damn I miss that look at her." He walk closer to the window. I had my back turned and started lotion my body down. I got up bend over and started rubbing my legs. "Awl look at all that ass she has no idea I miss her and want to make love to her."

He has no idea the wife is standing right behind him. "Is this the reason you don't want to fuck me?" He quickly turned around. How long you been standing behind me? "It doesn't matter. I have given this marriage all I can give. And I can't fix it by myself. I can see that's who you want well you know what Antonio go to her. I don't want you no more I can't make you want me or love me. So if a hoe is what you want. Go to your bitch." It's not what it seems like I walked into the bedroom looked out the window and I seen her. "Well why come you didn't close the fucking blind then." I couldn't. "Until you ready to fix this marriage I'm going back to Dallas." I'm trying. "How in the hell you trying and you sitting here watching this bitch naked. You know what Antonio when you want to fix this let me know. When you want to see your kids call me." You are not going to take my kids from me. She got dressed and started throwing some clothes in a suitcase. So you just gone walk out the door just like this. "I'm the only one trying to fix this you too busy watching the hoe next door ass naked. You come home from work I fixed a candle light dinner, something sexy as hell on and you don't want to touch me or make love to me." That's not what it is I'm tired. "Well your ass not too fucking tired you can watch this bitch here naked." He grabbed her and throw her on the bed and started fucking her.

After I finished greasing my body down I walked toward the window I could not believe what the fuck I am seeing. This bitch fucking his wife with the blinds open so I could see him. I was so pissed I got into my truck went into the gym and worked out to blow some steam off.

Is this what you wanted for me to fuck you? "Yes it took your ass long enough. I don't know what was going on through your mind when you was fucking me it must have been some good shit cause you ain't never fucked me like that." He just looked at her. Well I'm going to take a shower so I can lay down. When he got up he notice the blind was wide open. He walked into the bathroom got into the shower. Damn I hope she didn't see us fucking if she did I know she pissed as hell right now. My wife have no idea she got the dick that good cause I was thinking about Shekela what am I going to do. I want to make love to this woman so freaking bad. It is like I'm fining for her.

After I left the gym I went by the store to pick up a few things. As I was putting the bags in the truck. "Hey beautiful." I turned around. "You remember me?" Um should I know you. "You had a barbecue a while back ago and you invited me and the only reason I didn't come because you told me you had a boyfriend. I'm Tyrese." Oh I remember you. "It's been a long time." Yes it has. "So do you still have a boyfriend?" No I don't. "Now maybe I could take you out to dinner." Maybe. "So you gone give me your phone number again." What happened to the first time I gave you? "I lost it but this time I won't." Well here is my number give me about an hour and call me. "I'm gone do that."

After I left the store I went home. As I was getting the groceries out the truck, Antonio was walking out the door to take the trash out. We looked at each other. "Shekela I love you." Antonio fuck you and walked in the door. When he turned around to walk back in the door, the wife was standing right there. "You love her huh?" They just looked at each other. I'm going to sleep.

I went into the kitchen and made me a salad. After I ate I took a shower about ten minutes later my phone rung. It was Tyrese. "Is this a bad time." No you're actually right on time. "So what are you doing?" Just jumped out the shower. "Do you want to do dinner tonight?" I'm sorry I just finish eating a salad and honestly I'm about to go to bed because I got to get up early in the morning to go to work. "What kind of work you do?" I'm a nurse. We talked about twenty minutes after that I got in the bed. Tyrese sent me a text and asked me what hospital I work at so he can come by and see me tomorrow. I text him back and told him. After we sent each other a couple of texts I turned off the light, rolled over and I went to sleep.

The next day Tyrese came to the hospital to see me. We were standing in the hallway laughing and talking. Antonio walked up. He spoke we spoke back. He stood there pretending like he was looking for some papers. While me and Tyrese was sitting there talking. "So you gone let me take you to dinner tonight?" Sure why not. "What time should I pick you up?" About seven o'clock. "Well I will see you then." OK.

After Tyrese walked away "I guess that is your new play thing." Why is it any of your concern. "What did I tell you nobody is going to get my pussy." I looked at him. Did you and your wife have a good fuck yesterday. He looked. I walked away. "Shekela" He walked behind me "That didn't mean shit to me. Are you going out on a date with him to make me jealous?" This doesn't have anything to do with you anymore. And I wish you would leave me the fuck alone. I'm trying to be professional about this situation. I'm only talking to you because I'm at work outside this job don't say a motherfucking word to me. "You can say what you want to say, I'm not gone let you leave me." Well you know what Antonio it's too late I'm moving on with my life. And I suggest you do the same damn thing awl my bad you did that with the wife. "Are you gone fuck him?" Maybe maybe I won't. "Don't do that." Maybe I should do what you did leave the blinds open and let you watch me fuck him like I used to fuck you. "If you want to start a motherfucking fight you do that bullshit." Awl you gone come to my house and fight him. "You think I won't you fucking try me." And what you gone tell your wife. "Fuck that try me and see what's gone happen Shekela. Don't test me." And who in the hell you suppose to be? "Your man." My used to be man. Maybe I will fuck Tyrese tonight. And let you watch, suck his dick like I used to suck yours. "I tell you one thing Shekela you ain't seen the other side of me but if you pull some bullshit like that tonight you gone see another side of me you never seen before and it ain't gone be nothing pretty." Is that a threat? "Take it anyway you want to but I advise you to tell your friend Tyrese to stay his motherfucking ass at home tonight because you might have company at your house." Tyrese is my company tonight. "Well you know what you better cancel that shit. Because I will be at your backdoor tonight." If you come who to say I'm gone let you in? "Trust and believe me you want me just as bad as I want you." He walked away. You bring your ass over my house tonight to get some pussy I got a treat for your ass. I text Tyrese and told him tonight I can't make it something came up. He text me back and said "OK maybe tomorrow night.

After I got off from work I went by the mall and bought me something sexy to put on. When I made it home I went upstairs and the first thing I did went into my night stand draw pulled out an condom got a pin and poke holes all through it. Since he so devoted to his kids and I can't let him go I might as well give him a baby as well. I'm gone sit this condom right on the night stand. Because I know he is coming over tonight. There's no doubt in my mind because he think I'm gone give the pussy to somebody else.

It was about six forty five he called his wife and told her he was gone be late. "How late we talking about?" I don't know but I will call you later. "Are you coming right home from work?" Yes I am.

After he left the hospital. If she think I'm gone let this man here get my pussy she must be crazy. He parked his car a block from the house. As I was getting ready to walk downstairs I grabbed the condom just in case we don't make it upstairs, I better have this bitch her on hand. As I was walking downstairs I heard a knock on the back door. I smiled. When I open it. What are you doing here? "I told you I was coming over tonight." Antonio go home. "What you doing dressed all up for him?" Because I told we are going out to dinner. "I told you to cancel that dinner, because I was coming over." I know what you told me, but I'm not canceling my dinner. He rushed up to me and we started kissing. He ripped my dress off me. He picked me up and laid me across the kitchen floor, and started eating my pussy. I spread my legs wide open. I began to grind my pussy in his face. I was moaning my ass off. Damn I miss this. Then I thought about it. Stop, stop Antonio. "What you mean stop?" I can't do this with you go home to your wife you chose her over me. Now go home. I got up. "Ain't no way in the hell I'm leaving here without making love to you." I don't want you to. "Yes you do if you didn't you wouldn't never open that door." I have a date. I have to go upstairs and change because you ripped my dress. "You ain't going nowhere." I started walking away. He grab me by my arm and started kissing me. "You belong to me." He quickly took his dick out. "Don't make me beg baby please don't. I got to have you Shekela." The way you did me you think I want to make love to you? "I can't live without you please don't do this to me." Got him just the way I want him. I started kissing him. "Damn baby I forgot to get a condom." Don't worry about it I got one. He took it out the pack and put it on. He laid me back on the floor and we started fucking. We took it to the living room. He lit the fireplace I spread a blanket on the floor. We started fucking again. The pussy was so wet the condom came off his dick. I don't have anymore condoms. "Fuck that this pussy so damn wet to my dick I don't even care no more. Fuck me baby make me nut in that pussy." After he said that I fucked him like I have never fucked him before. And I knew then we was gone make a baby. His ass moaned so hard and when he shot that cum in that pussy his whole fucking body just went to shaking. He laid on top of me and beg me not to leave him. "Just hold me baby never let me go. Because I'm not gone never let you go." I laid there with a smile on my face. After he finally got up he laid against the couch and looked at me. "I'm so sorry for hurting you. I never met to leave you." So tell me Antonio where do we go from here? "I got to follow my heart and my heart is with you. I can't stay away from you and she know that." I laid in his arms. "I want to spend the rest of my life with you Shekela." I feel the same way. "Could you ever forgive me for what I put you through?" I can forgive you but don't never do it again. "Trust me baby girl it ain't gone be a next time because I'm going home and I'm gone tell her the truth." And what is the truth? "I'm leaving her. I know she gone do everything she can so she can take my kids away from me." She can't do that you are those kids father. "My dad told me to follow my heart. And that's what I'm gone do. I should have been honest with her from the get go and told her I was gone leave her but she threatening to take my kids away from me. That's why I chose to be with her. She went through my cell phone and seen all the text we sent each other the naked pictures. She seen me in the window watching you butt naked." When? "A few days ago." That was the same day I seen you and her fucking. "I only did it to shut her up. But the whole time I was fucking her I was thinking of you." I want you to be sure Antonio this is what you want to do walk away from your marriage. "I have never been sure of anything in my life she know it's over I told her the only reason I married her was because she got pregnant." You told her that? "It was the truth." Do you love me? "With everything in me." Stay with me tonight and make love to me all night long. "That's what you want?" That's exactly what I want. We got up went upstairs and took a shower together.

She had him paged at the hospital. The nurse told her he left hours ago. She looked out the window. Her truck is there. She grab her keys and started riding around looking for him. On her way back home she spotted his car a block away from the house. She put two and two together and figured out where he was. We was sitting in the kitchen having dinner talking. My door bell rung. Who can this be this time of the night? I didn't have nothing but a robe. When I open the door it was his wife. "Do you mind telling my husband to come to the door." Antonio heard her voice and came to the door. "I had to see for myself and now I do." I was gone tell you in the morning. "In the morning? You plan on spending the night here with her and I live right next door. You know what you two belong together. I don't even want to fight you Shekela. Because I can see he made up his mind who he want to be with." Mariah I don't want to fight you either. "The lease you could have did was came home and told me it was over." She walked away. I looked at him. Go talk to her.

After he got dressed he went home and tried to talk to her. "I don't want to hear it there is nothing for us to talk about." Where are you going this time of the night? "I'm going to Dallas." Mariah it's late you don't need to be driving on that highway. "Why do you care?" Rather you believe it or not I do you are the mother of my kids. "You know what? I'm so sick and tired of hearing that shit there. It's like you rub it in my face like you don't want me you just tolerate me because I am the mother of your kids. You say you a man prove it to me then. Tell me the fucking truth. I don't want to hear no more lies from you Antonio, I'm sick of them." The truth is I love her. I want to be with her I want out of this marriage. And I want to see my kids when I get ready. "You know what you can have out of this marriage you can be with her, but you won't see them kids until it's on my term. Why did you even fuck me a couple days ago? What was that about?" I got tired of hearing you nagging about it. "Is that the only reason why you slept because I was nagging about it?" I'm sorry. "You're right about that. You are a sorry ass man and I can't stand your trifling ass. Get out my damn way. You want her you can have her she is all yours. I will not fight over your trifling ass again." She grabbed her purse her suitcase stormed out the door, threw her suitcase in the car and she left.

He came back to my house. Is everything OK? "She left she gone back to Dallas." Are you OK? "Honestly yes I feel sorry for her but I'm happy.

I'm with the woman I love and want to be with and that's you. I love you so much you have no idea." And you know what you have no idea how much I love you as well. We hugged and kissed. We went upstairs and got in bed and started making love. The next morning we got up. He went home and started getting ready for work.

She drove all night crying because she knew her marriage was over. When she got there she went to his mom house. When his mom open the door she was crying. "Whats going on?" Antonio left me for the girl next door. "What when did this happen?" I been found out about them. "I am so sorry Mariah. When did you find out?" A while. I just didn't say anything because I was trying to save my marriage. "I told Antonio don't let that woman come between his marriage." His dad came downstairs. "What's going on?" "Your son done left his wife for that girl next door." "I'm sorry to hear that Mariah. Where is Antonio now?" I left him, and I'm pretty sure they are together right now. "And what are you gone do about your son?" "What do you want me to do?" "Call and talk to him and tell him to get his ass down here and get his wife." Don't do that dad because this marriage is over. "You just gone give up your marriage like that?" Mom he told me he love that woman, and that's who he want to be with. He also said the only reason why he married me because I got pregnant. "Antonio told you that?" Yes he did. "Lawd have mercy your son got some nerves to tell his wife some shit like that." He only told the truth on how he felt about me. "How did you find out they was sleeping together?" It's a long story and I really don't want to talk about it. Me and the girl already got the fighting. "Got the fighting?" I went through his cell phone seen all them text messages he been sending her. Telling her he love, he want to be with her, he miss her. She sending him naked pictures of herself. "That nasty hoe." She might be a hoe mom but he's in love with her. "So you telling me you not gone fight for your marriage?" What I'm telling you there is nothing to fight for. He has already made up his mind who he want to be with. "And what about his kids?" What about them? "Don't he know them kids need their father?" Antonio knows that. But he still choose to be with her. His mom got up. Where are you going? "I'm going upstairs to go dressed and I'm going to Atlanta and talk some sense in our son." As she was getting ready. His dad went upstairs "You not going to Atlanta." What do you mean I'm not going to Atlanta? Somebody need to talk to him. "Stay out of it." So you OK with him leaving his family. "No I'm not but he is a grown man. You can't make him be with nobody he don't want to be with." I'm not gone let him throw his life away. "He not gone throw his life away." How you know what he ain't doing? "When I went to talk to Antonio he told me he love that woman." And why you didn't tell me? "There was no point in telling you, because he ask me not to and the only reason I'm telling you this now so you won't go to Atlanta and get in his face about this. This has nothing to do with you." The hell it don't that's my son. "That's our son and he done made up his mind on what he want to do." Then what about our daughter in law? "I still love her but our son is happy with somebody else. Think about it look what happen to me and you what we had to go through to be together." She sat on the bed. You're right I can't make him love her. "If she makes Antonio happy be happy for him because if you don't you gone make him chose between you and that woman, and you don't want him to do that." You're right I don't. I don't want to lose my son. "That's why I'm asking you to stay out of this." But I feel so bad for Mariah. "So do I. But I love my son as well and if she makes him happy I'm happy for them. And I advised you to do the same thing. Be happy for them."

A couple of days later his mom called him. If you calling me to fuss and raise hell about what's going on in my life mom I really don't want to hear it. "That's not why I'm calling you." Because I know Mariah has been telling you everything that's going on. "She have and me and your father sat down and we talked about this. And he was right you grown and you make your own decisions. I can't make you love somebody I can't choose for you as well. If that girl makes you happy Antonio that's who you be with then." Thank you mom that's all I wanted to hear. "Do you love her?" With all of my heart. And she makes me very happy. "So what you gone do about your marriage?" I'm filing for a divorce but I am gone take care of my kids. "I know you is." I want you to do me a favor mom. "What's that?" I want you to get to know Shekela, because that's who I plan on spending the rest of my life with. "OK I will do that for you. I can't make no promises but I'm gone do that for you." I love you mom. "I love you too Antonio."

Chapter 9

As time moved on me and Antonio moved in together. I found out I was pregnant. We was so excited about that. He called and told his mom and dad about the good news. They was happy for us. Me and his mom is starting to get along well. Because we both love Antonio. My sister didn't think Antonio would ever leave his wife for me. But he did she got some issues of her own she got to deal with. Because she was involved with a married man and he didn't leave his wife for her, in her eyes she look at me as a home wrecker. But she will get over that. Kiera and Alexandria they are so excited for us. He finally got his divorce and we got engaged. We got to spend a lot of time with his kids. Mariah never accept the fact that Antonio left her for another woman, so she crossed over to the other side. She turned gay and got involved in a relationship with another woman. His family was devastated about that. Alexandria and her baby daddy got married. They had a little boy. When Chris found out about everything he was devastated with all of us because we kept it in the dark. But eventuality I knew he would cool off and he would start talking back to us and he did. I asked him would he give me away. He said yes. Everybody go together and planned our wedding. Three months later it was our wedding day. Everything was so beautiful outside the sun was shinning flowers everywhere. His daughter was the flower girl and his son was the ring bearer. His brother Pete stood up and sung at our wedding for us. My sister was my maid of honor. Kiera and Alexandria was my bride maids. After we said our beautiful wedding vows we kissed. People started gathering around hugging us and congratulating us on our wedding. We got together as a family and took pictures. Me and his mom took a picture together. After that me and my sister, Kiera and Alexandria gathered around and we took a picture. Something we would always remember this day because no one would thought I would get married. After we finished that the wedding reception was on. We got our eat on and our party. About two hours later it was time for us to go get ready for our honey moon. We was going to Hawaii. My sister and Kiera met someone at the wedding.

After we made it back from the honey moon, we went back to work all I did was work, sleep, and eat. And kept Antonio full of sex damn near every night. My time is here I'm nine months and two days over due. Me and Antonio just got done having some wild ass sex. We got up took a shower and got in bed. About twenty minutes later my water broke. He rushed me to the hospital. On our way there he called his mom and told them what was going on. They was happy. About three hours later I had a baby girl she was breath taking. Her dad couldn't take his eyes off of her. He was blown away. She was the most beautiful girl he ever seen. "I guess I'm gone have to get me a shot gun to keep all the boys away from her." I looked at him and laugh my sister, Kiera, and Alexandria came in the room with balloons, flowers, and teddy bears for the baby. Kiera and Alexandria was arguing about who was gone be that baby god mother. I said stop ladies let her have two god mothers because both of y'all are my sisters. We hugged each other. Antonio was taking pictures of the baby sending them to his mom. My sister had finally found love. I am so happy for her. Kiera doing her thing. Everybody was so happy, couldn't ask for anything more or better, but a happy ending and that's what I got.

I hope everybody learned something from this story. I sure did. You see ladies the little games I played with him, broke up his marriage that wasn't cool. I did it because I love a challenge and I always loved a challenge that's me being me. Being an X player sometimes a player get caught up and get their feelings involved. Don't get it twisted now even players get played but somehow somewhere I'm glad I had an happy ending. And everybody don't have an happy ending. One thing about a man, never ever say he won't cheat because he will. If the opportunity is there nine times out of ten he will take it. It doesn't matter what a woman look like because when the lights are off a dick will definitely come in place. And a lot of you sophisticated women who put on a business suit everyday and look down at women like me and think your husband won't cheat, girl please. Just because he's a doctor, lawyer, judge, or whatever never underestimate a player. I'm not saying all men cheat because they don't. I'm not even saying all men are dogs because they are not. Ladies we got to stick together some of us have to step our game up in the bedroom, because one thing about it if you don't take care of home someone else sure will, because everybody want a freak. And if you're not a freak you damn show better become one. If you want to maintain and keep your man. Because if you move next door to a woman like me and you ain't taking of your home, you see what can happen don't you. The only thing I'm saying ladies take care of your man. Keep him satisfied make his ass want to hurry up and get off work and come home and beat the pussy up. Guys I'm not gone leave y'all ass out now because if you don't take care of home another man show will come along and take care of the job for you. Because we don't want no lazy ass man in bed. We want a freak just like y'all want one. And if you ain't eating pussy you better get on your job. If you ain't sucking toes you better get on your knees. If you ain't hitting that shit doggy style you better bend her ass over. Maintain your bedroom as well. And one thing about us ladies we don't want no quickie shit. We want to fuck for a while. Make us cum six, seven, eight, nine times. Show us what you working with. Because if you taking care of home, home will damn sho take care of you. But one thing about it though people everybody don't cheat. Temptation is a motherfucker.

About the Author

I am Brenda L. Carruth. I am been once again giving you something hot, steamy, and erotic. It's been a while since I released a book. I am a mother, grandmother, and wife. I had something happen in my life that I had to take care of. With the grace of God he helped me get through all of it. God has brought so many special people in my life and I am forever grateful.

Dedication Page

One particular person in my life I call her my guardian angel, because she saved my life and her name is Ms. Virginia Cox. One of the kindest people I have gotten to know. Another special shout out to Kimberly K. I'm dedicating this book to all the freaks like me. Take care freaks I love you. God bless you. To the man upstairs who made all this possible for me without him in my life I couldn't do this. To my family who I love with everything. My friends who believed in me never once gave up on me. My fans I wouldn't be nothing without y'all. I love each and every one of you from the bottom of my heart. I appreciate all the love and the support that I get from everybody, and don't forget to check out all the books I got out right now. Shorty ain't hitting, Forbidden true love, Voices behind the phone, The other woman, A girl got to do what a girl gotta do. In stores right now. Keep in mind you will always get something fresh brand new.

Yours truly,

Brenda L. Carruth

I may be Away but
I'm Sure......
Even when We're far
apart, Distance can never
Change the Love
I have for You
in My
HEART

Printed in the United States
By Bookmasters